**PURE
SLUSH
BOOKS**

100
Lives

Pure Slush Vol. 20

First published as a collection November 2020
Content copyright © Pure Slush Books and individual authors
Edited by Matt Potter

BP#00100

Pure Slush Books
32 Meredith Street
Sefton Park SA 5083
Australia

Email: edpureslush@live.com.au
Website: https://pureslush.com/
Store: https://pureslush.com/store/

Cover design copyright © Matt Potter

ISBN: 978−1−922427−08−3

Also available as an eBook
ISBN: 978−1−922427−09−0

A note on differences in punctuation and spelling

Pure Slush Books proudly features writers from across the English−speaking world.
Some speak and write English as their first language, while for others, it's their second
or third or even fourth language. Naturally, across all versions of English, there are
differences in punctuation and spelling, and even in meaning. These differences are
reflected in the work *Pure Slush Books* publishes, and they account for any
differences in punctuation, spelling and meaning found within these pages.

Pure Slush Books is a member of the
Bequem Publishing collective
http://www.bequempublishing.com/

Dedicated to
DPT
who was there for #1
and has been here ever since

... poetry and prose by ...

Alex Reece ABBOTT • Sara ABEND–SIMS

Edward AHERN • Tobi ALFIER

Essam M. AL–JASSIM • Marwan F. AL–SHERIFFI

Elaine BARNARD • Priscilla BE • Paul BECKMAN

Liam J. BLACKLEY • Henry BLADON

John BOST • Howard BROWN

Pat BUBUL • Daniela BUCCILLI

David BUTLER • Steve CARR

Chuka Susan CHESNEY • Ane CHRISTENSEN

Jan CHRONISTER • Dave CLARK

Lisa COSTA • Anthony CRUTCHER

Francisco G DELGADILLO • Ruth Z. DEMING

Zélia DE SOUSA • Michael DIOGUARDI

Jacqueline DOYLE • Bina Sarkar ELLIAS

Michael ESTABROOK • Barbara GEIGER

Flemming GEORGE • JW GOLL

Ken GOSSE • Jonnie GUERNSEY

Chris HALL • Emmie HAMILTON

Mie HANSSON • Ryn HOLMES

Mark HUDSON • Sheena HUSSAIN

Phillis IDEAL • Doug JACQUIER

Joanne JAGODA • Tim JARVIS

Airea JOHNSON • Louise LAMEKO

Martha LANDMAN • Jim LANDWEHR

Ron. LAVALETTE • Christine LAW

... and ...

Larry LEFKOWITZ • Cynthia LESLIE–BOLE

Mike LEWIS–BECK • Christian LOZADA

Sally–Anne MACOMBER • Joy MAWBY

Jenean McBREARTY • Jan McCARTHY

Trisha McKEE • Barbara A. MEIER

Karla Linn MERRIFIELD • John MOODY

Allan Howie MUIR • Mark A. MURPHY

Remngton MURPHY • Kevin OBERLIN

Carl 'Papa' PALMER • DeLeon PEACOCK

Gary PERCESEPE • Matt POTTER

Harsh RAMCHANDANI • Colleen RICH

Leah ROGIN • Jennifer ROSE

Ruth Sabath ROSENTHAL • Rosie SANDLER

Rikki SANTER • Gerard SARNAT

Carla SCHICK • Sam and Sandy SCHUMAN

Iris N. SCHWARTZ • Mir–Yashar SEYEDBAGHERI

Beate SIGRIDDAUGHTER • Jonathan SLUSHER

Lisa STICE • David STRICKLAND

James SULLIVAN • Lydia TRETHEWEY

Lucy TYRRELL • Patricia UNSWORTH

Jill VANCE • Karen WALKER

Gertrude WALSH • Robert WALTON

Sarah WILLIAMS • Allan J. WILLS

Rita WILSON • Melissa WONG

Amelia Clare WRIGHT • Mantz YORKE

Welcome to *100 Lives*

Pure Slush was established in December 2010, on a whim.

I had been submitting flash fictions to websites and journals for six months: sometimes I was published, and sometimes I was not. And in that time, I had become increasingly annoyed at the approachability of some of the editors of those websites and journals. *No correspondence will be entered into*, some would say (or impart), and I had started to think I could do better.

For two months I thought about it … eventually settling on the name *Pure Slush* after watching gutters fill with swirling, dirty water during a summer storm.

What did I think I was looking for with Pure Slush in the early days? What is the website's philosophy? And is it any different now?

Well … it has always been about having fun, being amused, making connections with people, and amusing them too. Maybe making readers and other writers think or see things in a different (maybe unique, certainly fun and revealing) way. And doing it without a lot of bullshit. So the early motto 'Flash without the wank' fit well then, and even though some of our fiction (and essays and poetry now, too) may be a little longer than when we started, it still holds true ten years later.

In my day job/s, as a social worker, as an English–as–a–Second–Language teacher, as an early childhood educator, I love (and loved) hearing people's stories. Sometimes my day jobs are (and were) one long conversation about people's lives –

your life, our lives, their lives, my life, intended lives, disappointed lives, resurrected lives, happy lives, sad lives, normal lives, abnormal lives, extraordinary lives, humble lives, any lives, all lives. And it occurs to me as I write this, that really from day one, from story #1 published online on 6th December 2010, that's what it's always been about: celebrating people's lives, and giving us a window into different experiences and illuminating other perspectives.

That's online from 2010 to 2017, and in print (paperback and eBook) from 2011 'til now.

100 Lives Pure Slush Vol. 20 is not Pure Slush's 100th book, nor is it the 20th anthology published by Pure Slush.

In 2014, Truth Serum Press was established as an imprint for books written by individual authors.

In 2016, Everytime Press was established as an imprint for non–fiction books.

These imprints all now live under the umbrella of Bequem Publishing, and this book you're reading now is the 100th book published by Bequem Publishing.

And if you want to see all the books published by Bequem Publishing imprints thus far, turn to the back of this book.

Ten years is a long time for a whim.

So if you're reading this because you've been part of that whim, enjoy the book and the celebrations within, and thanks for joining us.

Matt Potter, editor and publisher

November 2020
Adelaide, Australia

Poetry

Catriona the Blind Woman Taste–Tests Whiskys in Tobermory

Tobi Alfier

Everything filtered through the scent of the sea,
the smoke of cruise ships, perfume of passengers
offloading for four–hour "buy everything tours",
crinkly smell of barnacles on well–worn ferries,
and the sky. The essence of bottomless blue.

Catriona knows well these don't count, but loves
to have them described to her, especially the weather
and the violet–gray color of the clouds.
She loves to know if they look angry like winter,
or tame and gentle as all other seasons.

She gauges her audience by the murmurs under
folk songs, sung years ago, recorded and played
for ambience. She sits at a small table,
five glasses and five bottles before her,
commences the taste–test for her own amusement,

a little tipple for her personal pleasure,
and the sale shoppes of local tradesmen—
no other reason. Oh—the smoky finish
of an Oban, sold on its land as well as the isle of Iona—
with a stately church, ploughman's lunch, and whisky

to finish—back on the ferry with a few hand–knits
and a few bottles, a lovely day. Catriona remembers
going there herself, the chimes of the ferry
as it approached the dock, the wind, sound
of children playing. She lit a candle there,

directed by the Priest to a votive,
his soft hand guiding hers, a blessing
only she could hear. The rich and enticing
flavor of The Golden Grouse, colored to match
its name. And so on. She ends with her favorite,

though Irish, Jameson runs in her blood along
with all memories of being young, driving fast,
living and loving, bound to a sailor who sailed on—
leaving her heart filled with dead butterflies,
her swaggering palate for whisky commendable.

Angler's Duet

Edward Ahern

Forty years ago, in a Newfoundland river,
I caught and killed an Atlantic salmon.
A hooking so elegant and a death so noble
That I became addicted to their pursuit.

But over decades their numbers shriveled,
blamed on netting, or on fish—eating birds,
or on seals, or on poachers, or on luck,
but rarely on climate and sportsmen.

I led hundreds of partners in death dances
in over twenty rivers before admitting
that they should swim away as unharmed
as stress and a torn mouth allowed.

But the salmon are dwindled far past
any help from my pyrrhic gesture
and the rivers run too warmly past me,
empty of the lives I'd treasured into death.

Alice, wife of Bob

Allan J. Wills

Alice, wife of Bob
Having specified
Her resting place
Beside beloved Bob
And space
Upon his sepulchre
For a brief biography
Alice opined,
'This stone is too small
For the important things
I hope you think of me
Dear children'
We replied,
'Love
Will fill that space'
For you are loved
Unconditionally
With all your flaws

Forgiven
Rest peacefully
Be free
Of burdensome memories
Slip free
Of your grudges
And vendettas
We remember
And let the cherished
Happy times prevail

Death of a Cat

Carl 'Papa' Palmer

the sodden broken body of matted black hair
my wife's once overweight cat, Max,
lies face down strewn at street's edge
against the curb of the roundabout
at the bottom of our hill

solemnly returning with rubber gloves, shovel,
burlap sack and cardboard box
removing the deceased pet to our backyard garden
the chosen plot a desired point for proper burial

never my friend always under his glare
now saddened by the sudden demise
already feeling his absence
the ever obvious resentment
of sharing his house
with the woman we both adore

I tearfully dig his grave
lift his body to lay him to rest
his claw catches in the fabric of the sack
Max had been de—clawed years ago

turning the lifeless head
looking into the closed feline face
exclaiming silently, *THIS IS NOT MAX*

after replacing the dead cat
to its original point of departure
my mission hopefully unobserved
I return to the house
to fill in the unneeded grave

looking up I see Max watching me from the hedge
however now with a look of acceptance in his eye

Bernard Buffet

Henry Bladon

(1928–1999)

(L'homme Témoin)

Wrapped in the long coat.
Pale and stripped back
like the winter willow.
Hollow. Sinister. Jagged.

The Witness.

Existentialism's poster–boy
takes his rectilinear angularity
and depicts the post–war misery
he sees around him.

Frenzy.

Compulsive energy
and chaotic creativity
through alcohol haze
create canvasses of frenzied angst.

A lost love.

Then the sad face of the clown
who doesn't understand
those sinister shivers in
the company of silence.

The party people arrive.

Moments to cherish
when chaos and creativity
enter into dreams
of triangular shapes.

Fragility.

Ejected from the throne and
cast aside by capricious critics.
A retreat into isolation
dragging a bruised reputation.

Vive l'art.

The cadaverous people, the toreadors,
the coffee pots, the dour street scenes
and the vibrancy of flowers.
The paint will never dry.

Roy

Jim Landwehr

I never knew you
but Mom always said
that you loved your kids.
I'm going to have to
take her at her word.

I never knew you
because you bowed
out before the main
event with me.
What would it be?
Camping at Glacier?
Doing 100 in your Pontiac?
Hugging me at graduation?

You never knew me
but I don't fault you entirely
most of it falls
on the murderous hands
of those who didn't
know you either
your messages to me
written in your blood.

Some day we'll get
to know each other again,
and, believe me,
I have much to tell.

Dante in Florence

Michael Estabrook

Ever been to Florence?
No?
We neither but we are here now
somewhere we've wanted to visit forever
but so much art!
impossible to know where to begin.

Brunelleschi, Botticelli, Fra Angelico, Filippo Lippi, Ghiberti,
Ghirlandaio, Masaccio, Masolino, Donatello,
Parmigianino, Andrea del Sarto,
Benvenuto Cellini, Raphael,
Leonardo da Vinci
Michelangelo

Dante Alighieri was obsessed with the number three
(and with multiples of 3), the sacred number: the Trinity

The high-water marks –
12 meters, higher than us –
on the sides of buildings
from the terrible Arno flood of 1966
the streets and ancient buildings filled with water
and a half million tons of mud

so much art submersed and damaged
we weep just imagining it:

Cimabue's *Crucifix*, a distemper painting on wood panel,
hanging for 700 years in the Basilica di Santa Croce.

Sandro Botticelli's *Saint Augustine in His Study* and
Domenico Ghirlandaio's *Saint Jerome in His Study,*
both frescos commissioned by the Vespucci family
in 1480 for the Church of the Ognissanti.

Donatello's stunningly realistic wooden statue of the
Penitent Mary Magdalene sculpted for the Baptistry in 1455.

Lorenzo Ghiberti's 20—foot—tall gilded bronze doors,
later renamed the *Gates of Paradise* by Michelangelo,
installed in 1452 on the east side
of the Baptistry of Saint John.

If I had been in Florence in 1966
I would most certainly have joined
the *angeli del fango*, the Mud Angel volunteers
who descended
on the city to rescue paintings and sculpture, books and artifacts
from the water, mud, oil, and debris stirred up by the mighty
river.

The *Divine Comedy* consists of 3 books, one for each of the
3 realms (heaven, purgatory and hell), each of 33 cantos;
Hell has 9 circles, Heaven has 9 circles; 3 beasts stand in
the way of his salvation, 3 guides lead him to salvation,
3 ladies intercede on his behalf . . .

Fortunately the Church of *Santa Margherita dei Cerchi*
remained undamaged.
I was especially eager to see this truly historical Dante building
erected in 1032. It was here that he married
Gemma Donati in 1285.
But more importantly, this is where he first saw Beatrice,
his lifelong muse and unrequited love.

The moment I saw her I say in all truth that the
vital spirit, which dwells in the inmost depths of the heart,
began to tremble so violently that I felt the vibration
alarmingly in all my pulses, even the weakest of them.

You have to be careful when on the Dante trail
(it has been 700 years after all):
there is little left that is real Dante
most of what is there is modern,
concocted in order to sell tickets
or trinkets or books or posters or drinks

The *Sasso di Dante* is the stone upon which Dante would sit
and watch the cathedral of Florence being built.
Seriously! A stone.
Like Plymouth Rock only larger.

He even invented a poetic form based on three.
The *Divine Comedy* is 14,233 hendecasyllables in terza rima,
3 lines of iambic pentameter, 1st and 3rd lines rhyming,
2nd line gives the rhyme for the 1st and 3rd lines of
the following stanza: ABA BCB CDC . . .

When lo! Love stood before me in a trance:
Recalling what he was fills me with horror.
Joyful Love seemed to me and in his keeping
He held my heart; and in his arms there lay
My lady in a mantle wrapped, and sleeping.
Then he awoke her and, her fear not heeding,
My burning heart fed to her reverently.
Then he departed from my vision, weeping.

Even Beatrice, his innocent unrequited love
has gotten herself imbedded in the tourist scene.
In her church there is Beatrice's basket
wherein lovers, particularly brides—to—be, leave notes to Beatrice
asking for her guidance in matters of the heart.
The basket sets alongside a lovely tombstone:

SOTTO QUESTO ALTARE
FOLCO PORTINARI
CONSTRUI LA TOMBA
DI FAMIGLIA
L'8 GIUGNO 1291
VI EU SEPOLTA
BEATRICE PORTINARI

21

PIETRA TOMBALE
DI

BEATRICE PORTINARI

(Under this altar built Folco Portinari family tomb's
June 8, 1291 was buried Beatrice Portinari.
Tombstone of Beatrice Portinari)

Of course she's not really buried here. Most likely she rests with
her husband's family in the cloister of Santa Croce Church.
But having her here
in Dante's church helps sell postcards.

I often went in search of her; and I saw that in all her ways
she was so praiseworthy and noble that indeed the words
of the poet Homer might have been said of her:
"She did not seem the daughter of a man, but of a god."

In fact, I am a bit ashamed to admit
I myself purchased a bust of Dante for 27 Euros
in the *Casa de Dante*
it will look so imposing on a shelf of my library
alongside my bust of Shakespeare

There are many statues of Dante (almost as ubiquitous as
Michelangelo Davids) throughout Florence. The largest and
most imposing stands out front of the Basilica di Santa Croce.
Here he looks stern, fierce and frightening like a conquering
general.

There is another statue of him inside the Basilica
di Santa Croce, atop his cenotaph (empty tomb – he's buried
in Ravenna) looking stern and fierce still, but also tired.

I was surprised to learn that Rodin's The Thinker
actually began as The Poet
representing Dante musing over his Divine Comedy
atop Rodin's bronze doors called *The Gates of Hell.*

It is difficult to imagine that this too was planned,
but Dante populates the *Commedia* with 3,300 people.
(Aristotle is mentioned more than 300 times.)

Arnaut Daniel, Bertran de Born, Sordello, Horace, Homer,
Lucan, Ovid, Juvenal, Boethius, Brunetto Latini, Guido
Guinicelli, Guido Cavalcanti, and Virgil – all poets mentioned
in *The Commedia.*

Today the original Thinker resides
in the Musée d'Orsay in Paris.
Other bronze casts can be found in
Zurich, Tokyo, Seoul, Philadelphia
and at the B. Gerald Cantor Rodin Sculpture Garden
at Stanford University.

Dante belonged to the White Guelph party (don't ask, it's way
too complicated) which was defeated by the Black Guelphs, and
he was condemned to permanent exile from his beloved
Florence (had he returned he would've been burned at the
stake).

Pope Boniface VIII, who exiled Dante from Florence in
the year 1302, has a hole reserved for him when he dies
in the Eighth Circle of The Inferno, damned forever for
the sin of simony. Doesn't pay to get on Dante's bad side.
In 2008, 687 years after he died, Florence
finally overturned Dante's sentence of exile
allowing him to return to the city of his birth.
However, Ravenna where he died
is not about to relinquish his remains.

Verily I saw and still have in mine eye
A headless trunk that followed in the tread
Of the others of that desolate company.
And by the hair it held the severed head
That in its hand was like a lantern swayed,
And as it looked at us, Oh me! it said.

The Ruin of Eleanor Marx

Mark A. Murphy

At the end of the small hours
walking
the solitary streets
dreaming our future without you

the fragility of our embrace

Our night dead mixing it
with your night dead
when the chips are down

Our night head conspiring
with your night head

whispering songs of starlight
and rebellion

Out of each song courage
out of courage song
joining isthmus
to mainland and bridge to bridge

freeing you from the analyst's couch
and unexpected
      abyss
baggage of morbidity
brittle glass of a would—be kiss

        ★

At the end of the small hours
you are alone
in the open window

borne remorselessly backwards
keeper of the *Nachlass*
keeper of fire and flame

part aristocrat, part Rabbi, part light, part dust,
part pain
a fern setting us free in return

unleashing spores in the night – enticing
igniting
with your fronds and ambiguities

        ★

At the end of the small hours
when the hand mocks
and the venal sun consumes

the last of the lunar night

When the bloodied nose spells indignation
upon the bed
When the shackled feet topple

all reasons for loving

When the fox in the abattoir
implies the fall
and the fallen star

When the hullabaloo in the theatre
reveals
only conceit and bluster

*

At the end of the small hours
when the candle is spent
at both ends

When the great relief of being
outweighs
unbearable lightness

When the pages are torn out of turn
and differences
of opinion
hide in the margins
like hieroglyphs on the temple door

When prophecy takes a dive
and the great arcana of history
      fall flat
When the aggregates are in

for the tenants in the slums
hiding coal for winter
transforming past into present

When the battle—lines are drawn
and choices must be made
Will it be fly
or will it be spider

         ★

At the end of the small hours
after the final joke
after the dreams of laughter

and forgetting

After the secrets have been dynamited
after the nails have been nailed
hopes palled

After the setbacks and flowering of doubt

After long convalescence
and the debt
never paid

After the nights of drinking
and fine—dining
with the *ingénue coquette*

After all the silence and waiting
and final act of caprice
After all the touching and tears

★

Come the night the world ends
we shall be waiting
eyes wide open

arms open wide

Uncle Bill

Jan Chronister

1955

I sit at his feet in the photo
big brother I never had,
sixteen years my senior
Elvis haircut, army green uniform
with "Price" on cloth tape over right pocket,
glint in his eyes like he's been places
done things, blood on his truck's
dashboard witness to losing
one of nine lives when he
missed a curve along
the Wisconsin River.

2006

At the Bayfield Library
a poet from downstate
reads, some inflection
reminds me of Bill.
I go to him after,
tell him he sounds like my uncle.
"Who's your uncle?" he asks.
Turns out he knows him.
Turns out everyone in Iowa County knows him,
even people in Dane.
"He's a legend," the poet says,
but I already knew that.

C. Gordon Tyrrell

Lucy Tyrrell

As September winds worried across the prairie,
Benton Lake, usually a landscape of water
with restively—feeding waterfowl,
dried in its basin like leftover oatmeal.

Snowpack had been slight, runoff slim, rain meager—
the news article said—managed flooding
too expensive to continue.
Plentiful wet, now parched earth.

★ ★ ★

Beyond the door of the hospital room,
my father lay with the sheets pulled up to his shoulders.
Sitting in the chair beside the bed, I counted his slow breaths.
Sepsis and pneumonia nudged him
toward his final breath.

A few days before, he drifted
in and out of consciousness—
like special documents lifted out
of a manila folder, then refiled.

His stomach drained with tubing,
the muscles to swallow beyond repossession.
Strong drips in the IV could not staunch
the bulldozer of death, terrible in his blood.
He spoke with words that came from beyond—
"I have seen angels, but I am not ready to die."

His mouth was dry.
My sister and I took turns wetting a sponge on a stick,
placing it in his mouth to moisten his tongue.
He asked for a cup of tea.
He could not swallow tea.

He lay there with death
foretold in the fierce quiet of breaths,
mouth open in sleep.

Now, I regret that I did not moisten
the sponge from a cup of hot tea—
English Breakfast—
flavored with milk and sugar.

★ ★ ★

Plentiful wet in the prairie lake,
parched now—waiting for spring rains.

The True Tale of
a Bear With a Bucket,

or Davy Crockett's Trustworthy Tale of an Extraordinary Encounter with a Bear with a Bucket Who Hails from Nantucket

Ken Gosse

From the Horse's Mouth:
"This testament, written both faithful and true
by the great–great–great grandson of someone who knew
an acquaintance who heard the renowned raconteur
humbly telling his story (sans hint of grandeur):
'The King of the Wild Frontier' from Kentucky.
His birthplace a bend in the Old Nolichucky,
the soldier, frontiersman, and statesman avowed
to the rabid attention of those in the crowd
at the inn where they gathered to listen and drink,
so attentive that not even one dared to blink
at this one–hundredth telling of such a wild tale
that it's not been surpassed by the captain's white whale.
His story: a stare brought a bear to its knees
while the woodsman stood still and as calm as a breeze.

This testament is, as I started to say,
an authentic account of his words on that day
with two verses appended, which seemed to be needed
because, as you'll see, it was never completed."

[The author's unknown and the date isn't clear,
besmudged by drunk fingers which read it each year.]

Where the Legend Began:
It was back by the Old Nolichucky
where I met a huge bear who was plucky.
I froze with a stare
till he wandered from there,
and I reckoned that I was quite lucky.

How the Legend Took Root:
They say that I spoke to the bear.
To be honest, I don't really care.
What crazy suggestions—
don't ask a bear questions!
That's not how I got out of there.

How the Legend Grew:
While wand'ring our western frontier,
I heard more of my story each year—
the tale of a b'ar
who had wandered so far
from the Nantucket home he held dear.

How the Legend was Preserved:
Once I gathered each piece that I could,
I decided time spent would be good
in rehearsing the tale—
they're a great trade for ale!
Here it is, far as I've understood:

The Bucket's Gist:
There once was a bear with a bucket
who wintered outside of Nantucket.
The lair was quite bare
but a bucket was there
and a blanket, beneath which he'd tuck it.

An Innocent Beginning:
The bear took a nap on a hill,
where he frightened poor Jack and Jill.
'Twas not his intent,
but downhill they both went,
and the bucket would need a refill.

Davy Sings the Blues:
Jack and Jill went up the hill
to fetch a pail of water.
A bear was there
and scared the pair!
They lost the pail Jack bought her.

The Best Laid Plan of Bear and Man:
A bucket and bear but no plan
(and no palindrome—search all you can).
"But what good would it do?"
"Why, of course! Hunter stew."
So he took it back home to his clan.

Strange Encounters of the Frontier Kind:
While heading back home from Kentuck,
the bear worried he'd run outta luck
and meet Davy there
who would give him "The Stare!"
then he'd say, "That's a pail, ain't it, Huck?"

The Way to a Bear's Heart:
So this big dumb ol' bear with a pail
came up with an int'resting tale
'bout a man from Nantucket
who'd just filled the bucket.
Nice snack with a chaser of ale.

A Rumor Can Outrun a Bear:
"There once was a man from Kentucket
who stared down a b'ar with a bucket.
Dave said to him, 'Smokey,
perhaps this sounds lokey:
Did you eat a man from Nantucket?'"

Chug–a–Lug, Chug–a–Lug:
That's where his narration suspended—
a tad short of where he intended.
Each verse meant a slug
must be shared from a jug
till the speaker and fans were upended.

What Happened Next:
Though the answer, delectably gory,
became part of the bear's repertory,
the great storyteller
Dave Crockett, fine feller,
ne'er told us the rest of the story.

Jacky

Priscilla Be

You decided to die
which I thought was a noble decision
considering the age,
you were 24 and it was 1980
and being a serious punk rock artist and all
I thought it was blazing courage.

Now I look back and think
how sad, you gave up.
You could have hung around for another year.
The cancer was aggressive
but you had some good drugs
you might have made a go of it against all odds.

I know now what a year can bring.
I know what I would miss.
I cling on to this life
like Tarzan to his vine.

Monsieur Bem

Sheena Hussain

Free.
Man of bohemian
is the celestial sky fleeting
Above the desolate wilderness

He stands, nearing the very edge
feet clawed;
tickled by beard moss beneath,
Bathing his regrets

Dappled thoughts
on a whim take hold blithely
Intellect—
gone.

Affairs with foreign lands, books
dreams unearthed;
A wild flower
held close

encroaches,
bleakness regresses.
Vociferous babbler chimes the wind
Free. He is…

He is no B.E.M, British Empire
Medal, his blood, partial polish
Life beckons
Impediment.

The hands refuse to embrace,
Life, love, the sacred truth
All he knows —
Is C.A.N.C.E.R.

Poem for My Grandfather Willie Catchings

Anthony Crutcher

Mama use to talk about you
And superman became real to us.
You lived in a "mule die buy another
Nigger die hire another" time;
Sweating, bleeding, struggling
Only to enrich the red clays
Of Georgia.
(I often wondered how it got that color.)

Left Georgia for the Tennessee hills
And a better life
Only to find the red clays of Georgia
Covering the slopes.
You lived in a time when "above average
For Colored" euphemized Black
Superiority.

So you sowed your seeds
In the rich red clay
To watch them grow,
To help them grow
And blossom another day,
To reap the joys
Of seeing you
Continued in us.

Louis Slotin

Mantz Yorke

You assembled the core for Trinity –
that first atomic bomb burst in the desert –
and had been awarded lapel pins
because you'd helped open the doors
for Little Boy to fall on Hiroshima
and Fat Man on Nagasaki.

Nicknamed *chief armorer of the US*
for your expertise in constructing bombs,
you carried on experimenting
('tickling the dragon's tail', colleagues said),
easing hollow half–spheres of beryllium
around a plutonium core
so reflected neutrons could edge fission
towards criticality – a risky procedure,
riskier still when you used a screwdriver
instead of the customary shims
to keep the beryllium shells apart.

The screwdriver slipped:
the beryllium bivalve clammed shut,
a chain reaction ran amok,
and the watchers' eyes filled for a moment
with blue light. Straightaway
you wrenched the shells apart – too late
to prevent the burst of radiation
giving you three–dimensional sunburn
and silently pronouncing sentence
on your recklessness: life,
to be served for a mere nine days.

Louis Slotin, a Canadian physicist, died on 30 May 1946
from the radiation released in this accident.

My Publisher, the Shithead

Sally—Anne Macomber

The Shithead emails in desperation.
I need a four—pages—long poem, he types,
for an anthology I'm putting together,
because another poet has pulled out.

I need someone dependable, he adds,
not genius necessarily, a journeyman
(or journeywoman) who can pound out
the words when I say so.

There's a theme to the book (he continues)
and the poem has to be
four pages long. And I need it
soon—ish, preferably tomorrow.

Tomorrow? And why four pages?
(I've never written poetry before
but the idea of a four—page poem
has my creative urges thrumming.)

The other poem was accepted and inserted
into the book, but then the poet
didn't sign the contract agreement.
Didn't respond to his sending six emails.

Now there's a four—page hole in the book.
The Shithead sends me some guidelines.
The poem does not have to rhyme
all the time, at the end of every line.

But please don't have para—rhymes
and internal rhymes and some rhymes
and half rhymes and no rhymes
and mega—rhymes and bum rhymes.

Above all: Please be consistent.
                          And don't use odd word placement.
          Odd placement   causes havoc   with rhythm
                    and is endlessly tiresome when format—
                                                    —ting.

Don't use big blank spaces either,
it chews up space on the page,

makes it look like you don't have enough
words and ideas to fill the space properly.

Don't use ★

or ★★ or ★★★

or ★★★★ or …

or • or ~ to separate sections too often.

(So, ★

★★ ★★★

★★★★ …

• and ~, I think!)

And don't use adverbs foolishly,

recklessly, or write lines that are way

way way way way way way way way

waaaaaaaaaaaaaaaaaaaaaaaaaaaaaaaaaay too long to fit onto the page.

If you're a young woman I'd tell you

don't write about love nor be married

to every word so my suggestion

of cutting just one sends you spasming.

Don't use long words no one understands.

That = objects and *who* = people.

Strong meter throughout or never at all.

though you don't have to start every line with a capital.

Other evils are bad punctuation, half–punctuation,

old men who think they're Hemingway, poor spelling,

no spelling, a mix of UK and US spelling,

and the Shithead simply cannot, *will not*, <u>*won't*</u> abide

widows

or orphans.

Airea's Montage of Mourning

Airea Johnson

3 packs of Camels in a week
Entire bottle of Barefoot
Drunk call to an ex lover
Unprotected drunk sex
Hangover next day encounter
Stale cigarette breath morning after
Plan B and Wawa iced coffee
Screenshots from last week
Apology drafts in iPhone notes
Conversation about expectations
Grieving Spotify playlists
Panic attack in Gainesville
Posts about sucking dick for a reaction
Saltine and salami dinners
Diluted lattes on tap
Melatonin induced nightmares
Phone call with my therapist during a plague
Eulogy to *lonely* written on a gum wrapper

Frances Marie

Barbara Geiger

My hand rests in your lap,
where once you rocked me close,
singing sweet melodies,
whispering of your love.

Once—smooth skin now etched with age,
my fingers curl protectively around yours,
interwoven like framed memories
displayed along bureaus and walls.

Your chestnut eyes search mine
for answers to questions
you no longer know how to ask.
Weary, they close to rest.

Identical eyes, ninety years earlier, peer through sepia haze.
Stocking—clad legs straddle an arm post
of a child's rocker, tiny hands clutching the cloth doll
your mother sewed for her only daughter.

Across the room, older brothers pose in military dress:
Earl, the academic and Albert, the jokester,
responsibility and fun shaping your world view,
like my two brothers – your sons – helped shape mine.

Tall and thin, dressed in poufy sleeves and hair ribbons,
you smile at me through photo collage windows
with your Boston Terrier, Saucy, Bup–Bup, your pet red hen,
and forever friend Alberta, keeper of secrets and dreams.

You stir, releasing my hand,
eyes attentive, energy renewed.
"Hi, Mom," I say. "It's so good to see you!"
A faint smile and nod sustain my hope.

Our souls will always be connected.

I brush the fine, silver hair from your face,
revisiting stories of family times
that taught me to appreciate my world,
love others and always, always keep learning.

Paging together through the family album,
you silently touch the faces and smile at the children.
I wonder what thoughts you have –
which memories you keep.

I thank you for raising me with such love,
an example of compassion and service
and bringing me, through faith, to baptism
into the Family of God.

I wipe away tears to offer a parting hug.
"You know that God loves you, right Mom?"
More certainly than anything you've done all day,
You reply, "I know."

And more certainly than anything,
I know we'll be together again.

Ode To Diana Haghighi

Mir—Yashar Seyedbagheri

we took to five—dollar movies, Diana and I
slipping Skittles, stealth spies through long halls
partners in crime, friends
she relished the roughness
of people kicked in the balls, blown up
action was high—octane caffeine, psychological films a treat,
like nesting dolls, how hypnotized she was
but she laughed at Jason Statham claiming to drive
a car on top of a train while on fire in *Spy,*
and rip off an arm with his other arm

Diana and I took to the streets
between movies and on weekends
cruising the wide swaths of street
in pursuit of new meals to try Mexican
Chinese today, Japanese tomorrow, what's new, she asked
or dollar drinks at Sonic, McDonald's, even a simple Diet Coke
walkabouts she called these ventures,
meant for sunlit days, but also rainy afternoons
after she worked for my father, the mustache man
worn down by his dissections, *you look dead. I want my taxes*
don't you listen, words assaulting with nasal noise
but she minced no words, dissected his lack of logic

and called him an asshole, while we traversed openness

refused to conceal disappointment when I failed to think
struck like a sharp knife, sharp
with love, when I didn't apply to a certain grad program
or look to the future
but she said so disappointed and then encouraged creation
believed I'd birth the world a book
turned keen eyes onto my pages
dissecting superfluity on the page like a corpse
what elegant cursive she wrote with
she could have been a president, a lawyer,

she could have been
a scholar, spoke of Nietzchian ubermensches
and anarchism and socialism
and Marxist theory and lamented
about the matter with Kansas, but history labeled her a mother
a former hausfrau, a secretary
to a mustache bristling who underpaid and overworked
but she took to the streets
the world taking and taking, demanding dues for her right to
live within spaces, but there was always a thriller
another miscreant being kicked in the balls
another day out
what would this day bring, she asked?

Bernard Herrmann: An American Prospero

Remngton Murphy

Then there's Bernard Herrmann,
Who wrote the scores for a plethora

Of classic Hollywood films,
Such as *Cape Fear*, *Citizen Kane*,

The Devil and Daniel Webster,
For which he won an Academy Award,

For a while he was Hitchcock's personal composer,
Giving us the willies with his hauntingly

Repetitive patterns, especially in *Psycho*
At the expense of poor Janet Leigh,

Always the perfectionist,
He demanded complete artistic freedom,

Always insisted
On conducting everything he composed,

In the '50s and '60s his baton turned mystical,
He evoked, like a musical Prospero,

An atmosphere of mystery and suspense
In *Journey to the Center of the Earth*,

Sinbad's Seventh Voyage,
And my personal favorite, *Jason and the Argonauts*,

In the Day the Earth Stood Still
He utilized overdubbing and tape—reversal,

Experimented with electrified
Organ, violin, cello, and bass,

Which had never been done before,
He blended the sublime

With a sort of spaced out cheesiness,
It was like Ed Wood meets Gustav Holst,

Panned by the critics,
Beloved by his many fans,

Including Beatles producer George Martin,
Whose work in 'Eleanor Rigby' is a worthy tribute,

Most impressive graffiti I've ever seen,
Spray—painted black on a concrete overpass

In big block letters,
BERNARD HERRMANN LIVES!

Dedicated to the SE section 34, Township 43–N, Range 19 W

Barbara A. Meier

Of this plot of ground,
facing Haw Creek,
the steadfast stones
in the family cemetery
hum of the vestiges
of lives lived on the prairie.

Of Valaria Ernestine Wacker
who told her granddaughter
of a story about bushwhackers
and raids on a farm in Missouri.
A dour woman,
a preacher's daughter,
never smiling, speaking
with German in her voice

the story told by her grandmother to her.

Of Wilhamine Caroline Tagtmeyer,
who married in 1863,
in Cole Camp, Missouri,
and lived on a farm,
in Morgan County, Missouri,
cattywampus from Little Dixie,
and next door to Benton County,

Of ruffians on horses, searching for whatever,
wearing their fancy embroidered shirts with long hair blowing
on fast rides and dismounts as they burned the barns,
raided the smokehouses, upending tables,
slashing furniture with cavalry swords,
storming a bedroom to flip the mattress for money or gold,
not seeing the baby asleep on top the patchwork quilt
of greens, blues, browns and rusty reds.

Of the heart of a mother fearing the silence.
Of saving the baby from a feather mattress soft in its suffocation
or to wait to watch the plunging sword, rip the feathers
into a drift of bloody plumes
The sounds of stomping boots, trailing flour and coffee,
killing the cattle for supper.

It was the civil war, border ruffians, raids, and skirmishes
on the Fisher family farm in the southwest
quarter of the SE section 34, Township 43−N,
Range 19 W.

I wonder why she told this granddaughter
this story. What I do know:

If you don't want to remember your grandmother's stories,
your own memories don't count.

When stories are not told, they become something else ...
forgotten. 'Sarah's Key'

The Life of Elvis Presley
(Why We Never Bring Him Back)

Kevin Oberlin

1

It matters little whose star is biggest
when each of us is up there somewhere.

2

They butchered pigs and smoked their loins
for half a day, then ate them by the river.
Memphis: America's Distribution Center.

3

What happens in Tupelo, nobody thinks
important enough to write about.

4

Prophets on the wireless called him
no more scandalous than Christ,
among us before we knew him.

5

When the ancients warred, none came back
except Odysseus, who you have to admit
took the long way home. But America draws
its heroes back. If he left a part of himself
over there, it must have been the same part
he left everywhere else.

6

He sat down and cried.

7

If you can name three movies in which he appeared,
I'll pay you five bucks. No strings.

8

If you have seen a movie in which he appeared,
you must bring a sack of pollen swept
from flowers planted with your own hands
and kneel before his altar. Dust the ground.
Mark your forehead. Dust the nose of any
who enters with you, living or dead, man
or woman or animal, flesh or spirit.

9

Johnny Cash went to the jail.
Where did you go?

10

When we picked him up the first time
he was high as a kite and wearing his fat pants.
We thought perhaps he'd escaped
his crucifixion. We brought him back
with pork and beans, with gamma rays,
with his mother's written permission.

11

Planet X—G7 erected a golden brick
eighty stories taller than the Empire State,
engraved on one side with logarithmic curves
to represent his lips, an anatomy jukebox.

12

The second time we filled a tank with water,
dropped him in and froze him, because he asked.
We remove him now and then for ribs,
and now and then he asks for his guitar
and writes a riff on being cold in space.
We never bring him back. He never asks.

GT

In Six Degrees of Kevin Bacon
say his name and see what happens.

The Artist

Mark Hudson

I was in my art class, surrounded by women,
who are usually the ones who take art classes.

They were talking about figure drawing classes.

One woman told a story, "When I was younger,
I took my young daughter to a figure drawing
class. I didn't realize the model would be nude.

"As the model disrobed, he had a shaved penis!
My daughter freaked out. She said, 'Mom,
we have to leave!' and scratched her
fingernails into my arm so hard I still have
a scar to this day! That was the end of my
figure drawing days. Besides, I haven't
seen that many penises in my time, anyhow."

One lady in class said to me, "I don't
think you should be hearing this, seeing
that you're the only male!" Ah, yes, but
how grateful am I that I got sex out of
my system as a younger man. Now I'm
forty-one years old, and I hear how women talk.

I once had a scholarship for figure drawing,
But I would never want to be the nude model.
My body is falling apart already. For me,
I will always be on the other side of the palette.

Dave the Tinkerer

Dave Clark

I am fairly comfortable with the man
I am. I just haven't felt much of a
connection to the general male
population. A distance from my own kind.

Many men seem to enjoy tinkering.
Tinkering in the shed, tinkering on
engines or with some house renovations.
I do and enjoy almost none of that.

Then after decades of feeling a lack
of common ground I realised — I am
a tinkerer too.
What I tinker with
is words.

I measure words and lines, saw them in half,
build them up. I renovate paragraphs.
I sand down and oil words to help a
sentence run smoother. My mind is a shed,

my man cave. I retreat into it to
work out and flex my creative muscle.
I can point to a poem afterwards
and quip, "Have a look at what I made, lads."

They'll probably welcome me with crossed arms
and say, "What the heck ya talking about?"
But deep down I'll know we hit common ground
and I won't feel so out of place among men.

My Names Speak Too Much

Christian Lozada

Christian:
>   more than the obviously heavy signifier,
>   defines me in relation to my alphabetically named brothers
>   (Adrian, Brian, me, Donovan)
>>   because Filipinos can't let a name be just a name
>>   they have to get cute with it
>>   I grew up with twins named Salem and Menthol.

Hanz:
>   like the promised land to a thirsty Moses,
>   hints literariness but for my white mom's illiteracy
>   Hans in Hans Christian Anderson is not spelled with a z

Lozada:
>   sounds ethnic

No One Could Say It Like Lady Day

Carla Schick

My dad drank scotch on the rocks,
same as Billie. When she asked him—
at the Royal Roost's bar
long before her final days—
What are you drinking, sonny?—
Dinah said, *same as you,*
Billie

The day she died, my dad was stuck
tossing out malfunctioning radio tubes
forced to watch a TV—like screen
with little green lines
to measure efficacy.

Break time   Outside the factory my father crouched
leaned against the dusty
brick wall & had a smoke

When the bell rang to return
Billie had been dead for hours
laid out in a New York hospital bed.

My father sat
on a hard bench
Twisted and turned
knobs with inaudible possibilities
of tones.   He witnessed
sinusoidal waves grow   shrink
Ascend
the scale   Listened
for intonations that met his pulse
halfway

      The day she died I was four
      He came home had a scotch
      followed by a beer
         a chaser

while they dragged her
         body from the hospital bed

Those men who tracked her down
the ones who couldn't fathom
her power
as she sang *Strange Fruit*
Black men's bodies
lynched and without question

The white men
who couldn't stand the words she sang
stripped her throat dry
cut off the methadone

Killed her   Crumpled her
body
Not just the liver cancer
cut off her methadone
in the hospital
just like they threw her in jail
years before when she tried to get clean

The day she died
my father sat on the edge
of his chair at the dinner table

Sang her words about lover men
and loss

The men who left her
didn't kill her

Couldn't bear her mournful
songs

The newsmen only told us
about her raw voice
the edge she had lost

My father shielded
His 78 rpm record
spun it round and round

Plucked notes
Reverberations
out of air.

Tony

Louise Lameko

As an engineer
he does not need to see a counsellor,
though often his family members do.
Apparently, the people in his household
lack the skills to master their own lives.

If only his partner listened more.
Then she would understand
the correct way to stack firewood,
and why extension cords must be wound,
not coiled.
In such order, peace is found.

Instead, the engineer's constant commentary,
like English subtitles in an English movie,
is rarely appreciated.

His family should give kudos
for the unsolicited advice
that is revered
elsewhere,
in places that matter.

August 1876:
Madam Dora DuFran's
Instructions

Karla Linn Merrifield

Take a bath, Calamity;
Wild Bill Hickok's back in town.
Scrub your cunny good.
And put on that orange frock
I laid out for you.
It's time to earn your bed, Jane.
Try to smile. Flirt with 'em.
No cussin', whatsoever.
No liquor. None.
First one's the hardest.
You might find you like it,
even if it's your bad luck
to be a lady tonight.

Because this is the big night.
Miners is gonna pour out
of the gulches—theys be three deep o'er
at Sam's bar at the Blue Union Saloon,
suckers pinchin' a few grains of gold
for whiskey and pussy.
It's our turn, it's your spin
of the gamblin' wheel to bet
on the guns and shovels of Deadwood.

To Emily

Lisa Stice

for Emily Dickinson

My friend who walks the shores of time—
you seem to visit me on the grayest days.

Just right of my heart, I keep a box
tucked behind my lung—The contents

sometimes rattle when I breathe. In this
box, I lock away the gray, news of loss,

smoke and tears. Here is the key—I trust
you to teach me how to release it all, write

it all out on paper to be hidden away again—
pain among the seeds, sorrow in the sugar bowl.

Emily Dickinson (1830–1886; United States):
poet (*The Complete Poems of Emily Dickinson*)

Mary

Jill Vance

A present of perfume —
did they really think the baby would smell?
Evidently expensive like nard oil,
used in special rituals by the elite,
not for frivolous dabbing on the wrists.
Squeezing up the stopper, she made a wish
to be taken to far—flung shores by the
scent of hibiscus flowers, but it reeked.

Who were they anyway? She didn't know them.
They advised going into lockdown now,
not for long, a while, a matter of weeks,
and prophesied that when it was over,
the whole world would be a much kinder place.
They left as she rocked her newborn asleep.

I Used To Be A Stripper

Ron. Lavalette

Three nights a week, midnight
to eight—ish (though I always did
my best to disappear briefly
on my 4:20 smoke break, or to
vanish altogether long before
the end of my shift arrived).

I always got paid exactly the
same, always the same exact
paltry pittance no matter how
much or little of myself I left
out there on the floor, no matter
if anyone was out there watching.

Stripping requires acid. I remember
I always showed up on time and
they always had the acid waiting.
I remember that when I was done
—hours and hours after my shift—
the acid just kept on working.

My Dear Fidel,

Gerard Sarnat

A half−century ago as an impressionable freshman med student
who burned his draft card while conducting actions
against the Vietnam War then hitching to Vancouver
to explore setting up a new life there

it was impressive that Garcia Marquez used you as an editor
I attempted to obtain a Cuban visa to study how − in the face
of Amerika's boycott − you could still build a world−class
model healthcare system serving everyone equally and well.

Over the decades, though I grooved Che's principled charisma
if not your too long speeches, it became clear from dissidents
segregated plus forbidden to talk with prying visitors, that practice
was − well − another matter: at first reality eluded me

since those Potemkin show villages were so well−stocked
with grinning plump pseudo−citizens not unlike how one sham
string quartet duped Red Cross inspectors at Hitler's death camps.
Totalitarianism got the best of Castro, but RIP, Fidel sure tried.

Gene Cernan, Astronaut

Jenean McBrearty

Gene Cernan communed with God,
though many don't know his name,
and you may disbelieve,
but he did it.
He gathered up his knowledge,
his courage,
his desires,
put them in a rocket, and secured them inside
the rocket's cockpit,
waiting for the countdown to uncertainty.
Did he fear?
No. It was just a trip to the moon,
like going to Cincinnati,
like riding a memory into the past.
Any hero could do it.
But to be the last to do it
was unlike the first '69 trepidation,
because it was filled with the sadness
of a dubious distinction;
absolute faith in engineering.

The challenge of conquest was fading,
Children can no longer seek experience
or hope or dangerous adventure.
They sit staring at pictures rather than look up,
and seek 3 X 5 inch destinies, and
statically virtuous,
never knowing the valor
of those who've gone to the moon
and lived to tell of their miracle.

The Snowdrop King

Rosie Sandler

In memory of James Allen, "The Snowdrop King"
of Shepton Mallet in Somerset, UK (1832–1906)

There is a breath–held art to this:
the peeling of petals;
dusting of pollen
against stigma.

His master eye has made
one hundred new milk flowers
and each one nods its greeting
to the breeze.

But then this dust:
innocent at first
as finely–ground flour
from his mill

– until it turned dark
as mildew and crept
from dying matter
into flesh.

And now the maggots in the bulbs.

Perhaps these plagues
are justly earned:
a punishment
for playing God.

He cannot know that gardeners
a century away
will plant one hundred
snowdrop types from his designs.

Only 100 Waltzed
that Particular Day

Ruth Sabath Rosenthal

inspired by Leonard Cohen's 'Dance Me To the End of Love'

The four violinists, a scruffy blank–faced crew,
played on — key players in a role they each knew
too well. With eyes, no doubt, avoiding the blankness
in those in the mass of confusion of trembling nakedness
feet away, the musicians didn't miss a beat, as brethren
lined up for a "delousing" shower; *after, they'll be given*
blankets, new uniforms, a mess hall where they'll be fed
a hot meal & fresh water daily; that, in a statement read
them earlier they couldn't have believed, not down deep
where terror must've been rising to the brink of leap;
yet numb they moved along to the beat of a tune, not one
of them had ever heard before — a tune, that procession
upon procession of more such beleaguered souls, too,
soon shall hear, simply because each was born a Jew.

Poet's Note:

In a filmed interview of Leonard Cohen shown at *The Jewish Museum* in New York City, U.S.A. as part of an exhibit: **Leonard Cohen: A Crack in Everything**, Leonard said (paraphrased): *The impetus for my poem 'Dance Me To the End of Love' had nothing to do with "romantic" love, or anything one would normally associate with "Love," but rather, how the Nazi SS routinely sought out musicians among the Jews in "extermination" camps—and had the musicians play during the process of their fellow inmates being ushered into the gas chambers.*

My Father, the Boxer

Martha Landman

in black and white, 1955.
The photographer shot from the left
zoomed in on father's righthand hook
his lightweight legs — no head gear.

I've never seen father box or asked
about the photo. *A total workout,* he'd say
but of all the sides of father's self
the boxer's the one I'd least expect.

When young, he gave my brothers
red boxing gloves for Christmas.
How I loved the fake leather smell!
I tried them on myself, played
possum when caught cold.

I watched father teaching the boys
the art of sparring, their plover legs
a bob—and—weave dance. The instruction:
hit on the gloves, cover the face.
I liked most the formal shake of hands.

There was a lot of head—butting
with father through the years.
He's not one to throw in the towel
or to stand in a neutral corner.
Words can knock you out quick.

Katheryn Holmes
– Peep Show, 1965

Ryn Holmes

The sky falls outside
flooding the street.
Nothing much happens
around here afternoons –
so it's slow and I'm bored.
Right now the club is dark
and stinks of leftover beer,
old cigarettes and sex,
riffs of loud music blaring
from the old juke box
in a futile attempt to excite the crowd –
so far just one fat guy.
He came in after lunch,
sits alone in the back, busy
doing something with his hands
I can't quite see
and don't want to.

I lean on this pole waiting
for an extra bit of business,
you know what I mean –

a lap dance with touching,
or even better,
some private "attention" booked
in one of the rooms down the hall.
The tips are usually good
when I offer a couple of extras,
but it's a real grind, you know?

The place is a dump, only brings in
old men with drifting memories,
the kind who survive on monthly checks
and look for a little sexual fantasy
away from their caretakers.
The others are mostly eager—beavers
from the Navy base outside town,
young men with strong needs for flesh
wanting a look—see
or maybe a few rough touches
on female skin.

While still a girl
without any real talent,
I hitch—hiked out of town to getaway,
love left behind in the rearview mirror.
Now I've used down my youth and beauty
giving intimacy and comfort to men,
but it barely pays the bills.

I'm so tired.

Mike Tyson

Sarah Williams

I knew at that moment
our love would never last.

Sitting knee–to–knee
eating Pret–a–Manger
in the afternoon sun.

Men in suits.
Mouthy teenagers with gold hoops.

Twenty–somethings on Roller Blades,
your eyes following the whipping of their hair
and the swaying of their arses
as they skate past.

Next to our feet
the guardians of Hyde Park gather.

Darting eyes and pecking beaks
grappling with falling crumbs
from your California Club.

A guttural sound rises from your throat.
Phlegm hits its intended target.
Feathers of blue and green, glisten.

Fucking rats with wings, you say.

Years later, when you turned to drugs
and I found solace in myself,
I read an article about Mike Tyson.

It said he was a pigeon fancier.
A pigeon was the first thing
he had ever loved,
until someone
ripped its head
clean off.

I wish Mike Tyson had been there at that moment.
Hyde Park in the afternoon sun.
I reckon he would have knocked you out.

Period. A Time in My Life.

Ane Christensen

No one will ever notice that I spilled my blood on the floor ...
That those darker smudges in the grass mat
Are not mere changes
In the natural pattern of dark and light

But are the excess of my nature –
The fullness of my body that fell
(That splashed on my feet)
Flowing over in the continuum that is my quest for me –

For my place in the world,
For my place among people,
For my role in humanity –

My body warmth,
My warmth of bodies:

My thirst for others who will look at me,
Will look into me,
Will allow me to look at them,
Into them and feel good, close and comfortable.

I had tiny red dots on my ankles.
They washed off when I sopped up the dark splatters on the floor.

His Way Was To

Rikki Santer

for Lee Alexander McQueen (1969–2010)

winnow through the cut, armadillos to anchor
bold fruit & smirk's purity. He cinched with a final
belt the knot of his notable, fragile buccaneer's
scent still nesting in the hides of his dogs.
Long live alien stilettos, shoulder beaks,
blood sighing beneath beaded tattoos.
Tight tight corseted bravado, far–from–fine
lace, the asymmetrical & the ravaged all luxed
for live performance. Opera in the next sequined
dress tarnished & distressed. Couture his anti–thesis,
sullen wings sprouted after a lost mother, his last
note blooming on a weary copy of *The Descent
of Man* fringed with orphaned threads, his riddle
for the bite & the bruise.

Another Man's Daughter

Harsh Ramchandani

When you take in a view of the city
you are gifted with endless stories.
of people living their lives naturally,
as if they were not being watched.

Stories from the office tower
that blocks your view of the harbor,
where when the sun goes down, faces emerge
from behind the mirrored panes of glass.

You learn how people on the fourteenth floor
have to stay late on Friday nights,
because you watch them waste their time
from Monday to Thursday every week.

And how the security guard has his dinner
precisely at eight o'clock every day.
It's difficult to tell what he's eating
but it looks a lot like yesterday's sandwich.

In the next building, an upscale hotel
teems with activity at every hour of the day,
its rooftop bar painting the sky above
in drunken shades of purple neon.

The windows below perfectly proportioned
to each hold its own biographical snippet.
Moments that are wiped clean in the morning
when the sheets of lust have been changed.

By the subway station stand apartment blocks
due to be demolished years ago.
Where people bring their stories home
to work on them, like a well−written book.

In one west−facing home a mother reads
to her daughter every night. And every night
when the lights are out and the night is still,
the father returns to the daughter's bedroom.

Granda'

John Moody

It's dawn, the mythology of childhood.
A damp pre−gender awakening huddled
for the comfort of an open fire.
Before brown speckled ceramic fireplace.
Ovens beside, spotted like leopard skin,
warming food; centre of family rhythm.

While Granda' forges his morning routine
before he heads for the anvil
of blacksmithing in the shipyards.
His irons festering in the fire.
Under the rhythm of his hammer
hot smelling salamander coals hiss.

He banks the black coal dust
which damped the overnight heat
and builds it up for the blaze.
His mastery of fire flaunted
for the boy, small runt shivering
sucking the heat to his chill.

Sprinkling coal like sacramental water,
shaking the grate, burnt cinders
cascading upon the hearth. He picks them
up, casually throws them in the grate.
Lizard−leather skin immune
to scar from decades at the forge.

Working−class Prometheus to worship.
The boy's prostrate under his Granda's
masculine pride
as Granda' takes his Adam's serpent out
and into the kitchen to let it grow and heat
in Eden, then to brew the morning tea.

Leaving an awe−full boy alone.
His heart pressed to black anthracite
fed grey ash as the substitute for an ingle
of orange love−embers.

Cashier

Melissa Wong

My eyes sum up the sleepy people standing in front of me
Wait, watch, it's my job to form a cold reading of customers
Psychoanalyse their unconscious thoughts and feelings
Because I am a tired cashier who works the midnight shift

My livelihood is at stake if I smile the wrong way
Smile, smile, because the customer is always right
I cannot afford to have anyone here file a complaint
Because some people seem tired and cranky at night

It's so busy my supervisor forgets my breaks sometimes
Food, food, everywhere and not a crumb to eat
It is not easy working at a local grocery store
When I get that break, I'm going to stuff my face!

"Oh, I think I forgot to pick up some hash browns."
Move, move, the lady sent me to fetch hash browns
I grab a bag and power walk back to my register
She didn't say thanks but might've flashed her teeth

The lady had forced a gentleman behind her to wait
Careful, careful, he wants me to fetch a different drink
He had a red soda but he wanted a blue one instead
I leave partly to get away from his dangerous mood

It's so busy I forget when my shift ends sometimes
Work, work, all the time and no time for a nap
My supervisor is shocked when I check the clock
Who needs a nap, it's past time for me to go home!

Afterward, I served a man who seemed to pity me
Smile, smile, as he leaves with his groceries
Because I met a nice customer on the midnight shift
What a nice way to end another long night!

It's a day in the glamorous life of an essential worker
Tick, tock, my shift ended an hour ago
When I check the clock, I'm always shocked
Remember to pay to me for that extra hour!

A Refugee

Sara Abend–Sims

Was he erratic kind of nuts
plucked eyebrows
gestures and surprising smiles
in rhythms of their own?

refugee boat person, he said
a lucky one before the new rules
he lived in fear in the old country
kept in detention in the new one

now he is free but his horrors
are dense — the new freedom elusive
no matter how hard it knocks
on the walls of his psyche

does he miss his old home
streets sunlight smells family
food, good times or bad
the religion that made him
different hated — a pariah?

I don't know if Tehran was home
when an adult or that he will
ward off the demons of his past
but trust that day will come

when he won't need to look around
then lean close and whisper
I'm a Christian, to the stranger
who sits by his side on the bus.

Because My Son Is White

Mie Hansson

Because my son is white,
I don't need to fear a cop's knee at his neck
He will live in a world with the law on his side
No prison—for—profit will be made out of him
When he applies for a job, he can safely enclose
A picture of his face and Caucasian nose
He knows without question it won't jeopardize his chance
His skin speaks louder than the way he can dance
I can sleep softly at night without a sudden call
By a cold voice telling me that a bullet has fractured his skull
Raised in a society that favours his kind
Old women won't grasp their bags when he walks behind
Young girls won't cross the streets when seeing him at night
The cashier won't hold his note up against the light
His white skin is his armour, he doesn't need weapons
Police brutality is something foreign he can't fathom
My son will not be incarcerated for smoking a bit of weed
Or end up on death row for a crime he didn't commit

If my son was black, and if I was, too
We would know a form of rage that few whites do
My son would learn self–defense and constitutional rights
For the uniforms would be at his heels day and night
Waiting for him to stumble then convict him of crime
Exploit him as a criminal to make the shareholder's dime
For once he is locked up, he can't participate in elections
Inside the prison walls there's no thirteenth amendment
My son would study hard but all in vanity, for in reality
A white kid with half his brain capacity grabs the vacancy
He would encounter this injustice again and again
While politicians are on campaign for the American Dream
But that was never for him, he has to try and make a living
Legal or not, the law is either way against him
I would attempt to teach him to be the bigger person
To respond to bigotry and systematic racism
With love that I hoped would crush the hate
But nothing can change the ways of the US state
Governed by corporations that profits from discrimination
Writing new legislation that stinks of segregation

I'll tell you what the justice system means to me
Mass incarceration of my people while
Monsters like TrumpStein go free
A racist runs our nation from the house of white supremacy
A sex trafficking paedophile receives unlawful immunity
While I get pulled over without explanation
The coppers talk to me like I never had a graduation
Why should I respect authority? Give me one good reason
All my life you've been an example of evil
My ancestors knew it, and we know it today
It didn't finish when you unlocked the chain
You find intricate methods to keep us down
Still patrolled by the crows that are flying around
You insult us in front of our churches
You allow disgraceful speech
You teach us the very violence you preach us not to commit
You are as much a joke to us as you are tragedy
That's why you see us laugh while tears fall at our feet
In our dictionary democracy means hypocrisy
And this brutality is just the symptom of a greater disease

My love travels deep, make no mistake
But touch my son and I swear your house will shake.

A Biker's Lament

or how Alf Smith of 22a Windsor Avenue,
London came to terms with his midlife crisis

Allan Howie Muir

Ah don't know where you get it.
The impression that ah'm wild,
Ah'm just a soft ole pussy cat.
Why, baby, ah'm just mild.

At parties ah get walked on.
The chicks they pass me by.
When ah start ma chattin' up,
Ah only gets a sigh.

Ah'm so boring fashion–wise.
My hairstyles are so fey.
Ah've grown it, shaved it, waved it,
And greased it to a smooth D.A.

Ah've worn the latest styles.
Ah'd say ah've got some verve.
Ma flares are real impressive:
Y'know, this man's got nerve.

One day ah found maself
At the motorsickle store;
Thought ah'd buy a motorsickle:
Larn the motorsickle lore.

Now folks pays me attention
With ma helmet and its horns,
Wearin' leather cowboy boots:
Oh ma God, they give me corns.

But when ah ride ma motorsickle,
And the wind is blastin' thru,
As rain soaks in ma underpants,
Ah do believe it's true:

When it comes to bein' manly,
Ah've found maself an'all,
Standin' in ma high−heeled boots
Is when ah sure as hell walk tall.

Ma woman she keeps tellin' me
Ah oughta give it in.
Says that tauntin' motorists's
A helluva mortal sin.

So ah'm hangin' up ma leathers,
With ma rainproof undies, too,
An' ah gave away ma helmet
To the wild animal zoo.

But now ma days are empty.
Ah don't know what ta do:
With no greasy motorsickle
Ah feel ma life is through.

Perhaps ah'll try hang glidin',
Mebbe parachutin' too
Or mebbe deep—sea divin',
Tho' ah could contract the flu.

So things is back to normal:
Commutin's such a trial,
But when it comes to danger
Ah'll try accountancy a while.

Daddy Wright

Amelia Clare Wright

I could tell you that he loathes IPA beers.
or that in his college yearbook photo he has a creepy mustache
or that his second toe is longer than his big toe.

I see my dad
in snapshots.

I see first
his ring that turns on itself.
I remember him having it as long as I've been alive,
fiddling with it during tv shows and concerts,
I see it large in my little hands,
made whole by his right ring finger.

I feel that ring still on my back,
his hands large and cool through my shirt
that one time I thought too hard about infinity
and had my first panic attack,
thinking the world was swirling underneath me.
I hear him promising where I am,
cold tile under my knees,
reminding me to
Breathe   Breathe   Breathe.

In this one, he is standing onstage,
a head taller than all the other singers,
and as he sings his baritone notes,
he scratches his nose,
and my sister and I swell with glee
at the secret signal that he sees us.

Here is one when I am eight and small,
and he is calm and tall and entertains
my friends by holding up his palm
and daring them to try to jump high enough to touch it.
Here he shakes his head as none of them do,
a wry little smile and a wink at me.

There I am, eight again, and he took me to work with him,
inputting data from a spreadsheet to Excel,
and he let my tiny fingers do it for him,
eyes scanning the document for little human errors.

And there I am, fourteen this time,
and he drove me to my job this time,
and I told him to fill up the tank before we left,
and instead we ran out of gas just as we pulled onto the highway.
There are a few more of these running out of gas snapshots,
but they are almost all adventures after the eye rolls.

Here are about a hundred of him
helping me with my math homework,
my watching him check it with his teacher's face on
and my hair wet and dripping down my back ready for bed,
and here's only one of him
telling me he couldn't remember the math anymore
and I would have to do the precalc myself
and my bewilderment at a man I swore knew it all.

Here are cabins in the woods,
here are dark nights of driving us home,
here's him picking me up from every playdate and party.

I see ones of him hugging my sister
and ones of him kissing my mom,
and ones of him scrubbing the dogs,
and there's one in there of the cat falling off the ledge into his soup.
So many snapshots of John as family.

I see here some beach days.
He burnt pink every time, never mind the sunscreen.
He would stand at the edge of the ocean,
only dipping a toe into the water despite our seaward pleas.
He was always on the shore,
always watching over us all.

Having Read
the Paperwork on
Henrietta Bettman

Daniela Buccilli

1.
Her lover writes to the Comandante in Rome:
She is a decent, respectable person. A gallant gesture
from Alfonso Lamagna – widower, textile importer.
A sweeping romantic. He brags about her in a way
that suggests old age: *a loving partner, but also a nurse.*

In his third letter declares his willingness
to be punished in her stead. He pleads for her release
from internment south of Rome. Jaded, middle–aged
divorcee swore a hundred times that chivalry
is an empty bag, I find him here on his knees in a file.

2.

Not yet fifty, fibroids in her uterus, she writes,
she has a doctor in Florence, an apartment, someone
to tend to her recovery. The State would have no responsibility,
except to grant her this modest medical leave.

How tender the fascists at the news of uterine pain.

3.

Dear Henrietta with the stupendous eyes,
what can you say about your first husband,
except that he did not kill you.

Mine pulled my hair when he banged my forehead
on the Silverado dashboard on our way to my surgery.

But neither you nor I die by their hands. So many
who did not kill us. The furious Florentine official
discovered your lie about needing surgery. You lay
three months in a bed with Alfonso – postponing,
postponing a hysterectomy, a team of doctors excusing.
On the slow train back, you stop in Rome to visit
Comandante Pennetta who files a permanent transfer request:

the heavy bombing & famine might kill you was the worry.
Curious that the Office of Counter–Espionage denies it,

it turns out, three times. Later, a soldier will accuse you
of being a spy. Then, you are killed at Auschwitz.

4.

I begin a romance in the village with an Austrian soldier.
The others will remember my evenings drinking with him.
Can you blame me? The war is not easy.
Didn't you love a man who wanted to kill you, too?
He still points to your life as proof of his blamelessness.
If he wanted you dead, you'd be dead.
We have no right to talk about him like this, he says.
We can agree boyfriends are not bodyguards.
Yours had you pray with a shotgun in your mouth,
promised to shoot himself after he shot you. Remember,
it was you who removed the barrel and left.

Paul Gauguin

Lydia Trethewey

Jacob wrestling the angel on a plane of vermillion
gold wings stolen from Japanese prints
nuns' heads bowed bearing witness to your vision

You once asked, where do we come from
what are we where are we going, and I
wonder, what would you hope for your legacy

First, a failed tarpaulin salesman with
five children and your wife winning bread
while you painted, before you left them

A cloissonist synthetist primitivist pastoral
painter sculptor ceramicist sadist your colours
lacked gradation on purpose, you were bold

Enough to forget the lives in your wake. *Yellow
Christ* made in 1889 shows a rejection of
Renaissance perspective but still, religion holds on

Yellow House in Arles is where you stayed
with Vincent, where his masochism
complemented your ego and when

You left him too, the agonised howl of
thin steel severing his softly lopped flesh
so he could no longer hear the memory

Of those nights you spent in local brothels
pretending not to know, his ear wrapped
in the daily news, keep him carefully.

Expressive painter you set sail for distance
for your next vision, spirit of the dead
watching your bride, thirteen and naked

Bare, was it subconsciously you painted
her legs fused together in fear, made
from mud with hands raised in surrender

Oil on burlap. Is she real or is the ghost
imagining her, your "noble savage" girl
wed in an afternoon and planted with

Your creative seed. She bore your child and then
you left, returned to France with paintings of
totemic women withstanding the entire world

Where did you come from? What are you?
Where are you going? Legacy in glossy coloured
pages, history lectures and the walls of the Louvre

Mi Abuela, Before

Emmie Hamilton

My abuela would cook for us,
every Sunday.
It used to be more when she actually lived with us,

but that was before…
and this is after,

when she was making plans to return to the island.
The garlic and onion would sizzle
and the smell would permeate
deep into the pores of the walls.

I loved breathing on those days.
I always hoped I was her favorite
but I was never sure,
because there were so many of us.

But I always thought she would hold me longer,
press me in so I could inhale her gentle floral scent
and shiver as her hair tickled across my face
like spiders gently weaving their web.
Her lipstick would always stain my cheek
a rouge that always seemed permanent.

She always seemed permanent.

Prose

Don Leslie's ChapStick

Cynthia Leslie—Bole

A tube of ChapStick accompanied my dad wherever he went, reliably riding in the right front pocket of his business—suit pants or his weekend jeans, depending on the day of the week. ChapStick was nothing fancy back then, no tropical flavors or lip—tinting colors, just a slim black tube with white writing and a white, no—nonsense cap. Its main ingredients were unapologetically petroleum—based, without the pretensions of jojoba oil or aromatherapy essences to appeal to back—to—nature sensibilities. ChapStick was proudly untrendy, a product a man could use without sullying his manhood or reputation. Many times a day, Dad would whip out his trusty tube, lubricate his lips with a practiced flourish, then slide it back into his pocket to await the next tour of duty.

For me, Dad's signature scent was the strange, waxy aroma of ChapStick. His kiss was a ChapStick kiss, one I relished every night when he came to pop me into bed and say goodnight. Often I could persuade him to stay a while, radiating subtle smells of ChapStick in the darkened room while he sang me songs with his warm brown eyes glinting from the light in the hall.

"*Skeeters am a hummin' on the honeysuckle vine, sleep Kentucky babe. Lay your little curly head upon your Daddy's chest, sleep Kentucky babe,*" he would croon with his version of a Southern drawl. Or perhaps if I was lucky, he would belt out a rousing rendition of "*I wear my pink pajamas in the summer when it's hot, I wear my flannel nighty in the winter when it's not, and sometimes in the springtime and sometimes in the fall, I jump between the covers with nothing on at all.*"

I particularly loved what I thought of as the naughty skinny–dipping song: "*Once I went in swimming where there were no women, down beside the sea. Seeing no one there, I hung my underwear upon a willow tree. I dove into the water just like Pharaoh's daughter dove into the Nile. Someone saw me there and stole my underwear and left me with a smile.*"

I also adored how Dad growled fiercely as he sang the Princeton Tiger song, but probably my favorite irreverent ditty was 'Sam You Made the Pants Too Long'. I particularly loved the line that went, "*I get the queerest breeze right between my knees. My belt is where my tie belongs 'cause Sam you made the pants too long.*"

I knew how to get Dad going and keep him going to postpone bedtime and savor his attention. He was a softy when he took off the mantle of executive that he shouldered each morning, and he was surprisingly sentimental for a titan of industry, someone in charge of other people's fortunes and lives.

When I experienced one of my frequent bouts of leg aches, the bones throbbing with deep growing pains, Dad would massage my legs while he sang, demonstrating the old Army trick of pushing the lactic acid up my legs toward my heart to lessen the ache. And when my legs weren't hurting, he sometimes read books like 'Stuart Little' or 'Winnie the Pooh' to me before leaning over to plant his ChapStick kiss on my cheek. And when he finally turned to walk from my bedroom,

I watched his back recede with a feeling that I had just been fed a rich and satisfying meal, full of nourishment for my small soul. I felt cared for and seen, blessed by having his attention focused only on me for just those precious few minutes before bed. When he said "good night, sleep tight, don't let the bedbugs bite" over his shoulder and closed the door, a waxy smear of ChapStick stayed on my cheek in benediction as I drifted off to sleep.

In the morning, Dad was different, but the ChapStick smell still marked him, an olfactory signature that stayed the same even as he took on a radically different role. On weekdays he emerged from his bedroom all business, wearing a suit, tie, and starched shirt, and he focused efficiently on downing his coffee and his unvarying bowl of Life cereal as fast as possible. I could see him preparing internally for the day, arranging his responsibilities in his mind and adjusting his professional persona along with his fedora and trench coat in the front hall.

Dad felt a bit more like a stranger to me as he set off for work, because unlike me, he belonged to a world devoid of magic, dress up, and pretend, but that only added to his mystique. And when he bent to plant his waxy kiss on me after picking up his briefcase, I knew at least part of him was still mine. I reminded myself that I knew secret, special things about my dad that people in the big, official world weren't privy to. I reveled in the fact that no one else at his vast company knew he wore boxer shorts with flying saucers on them, but I did. They didn't know his toes were short, stubby Tootsie Rolls like mine, but I did. They saw a mysterious different side of him and called him Mr. Leslie, but they didn't know about the close—up smell of his ChapStick. I did, and unlike them, I got to call him Dad.

Minia

Francisco G Delgadillo

I love you is a phrase we exchanged only once. Not when I'd leave home or come back from school, bullied for being a teacher's pet. Not when you left for the United States to take on seasonal work for months or returned home early because I had a toothache and was crying inconsolably for you. Not when your mother died unfairly young of cancer during my elementary school years, and I saw you crying inconsolably for her. Not when we said goodbye at the steps of the bus that would take me in my mid–teens from Mexico toward the United States on my own. You would only bless me.

You, the oldest of 13 siblings, resigned yourself to leave school after second grade in a rural municipality in Mexico to help raise the growing number of siblings as if they were your own. You often recounted with pride, even into old age, how you cooked, washed, and cleaned at home, and how you also worked the family's parcel of land, tended to horses, and milked cows. I, the youngest of six siblings, complained when I had too much homework or had to help with chores around the house. I graduated from college and have traveled around the world for business and leisure.

I love you is a phrase we exchanged only once. Not when I graduated with honors from high school or college in California. Not when I started my first professional job right after college. Not when you had to be strong for your siblings at your father's wake after his long dependence on dialysis. Not when I bought my first—our family—home in San Jose. You blessed me every time.

You married my father when you were 21 and he was 25, both of you surprisingly old for the times. I don't know why you waited that long. I don't know if you were in love before or during your marriage. I could never tell, and you never said so. You had my oldest brother when you were 22. You gave birth to my four older sisters and myself every two to three years. I'm 48 and haven't been in a long–term relationship. While I fell in love once, I wasn't loved back.

I love you is a phrase we exchanged only once. Not when you asked me with nervous vanity which dress you should wear after I was paged that a liver donor had been found for you, and we had to go to the hospital for your transplant surgery right away. Not when we drove back in silence that evening after you were sent home still with your ailing liver because the donor was not, after all, a match. Not when you finally received a liver transplant years later at Stanford Hospital. Not when I earned a job promotion or opened my own business. Not when you would brag about me to family and friends or even strangers. You blessed me time after time.

You wanted me to have children. But you stopped asking me when I was going to marry once my youngest sister married 17 years ago. At the time, I told you to make sure you enjoyed the wedding, for it would be the last one in the family, unless someone remarried. To add an exclamation mark to my declaration, I colored my hair platinum blond the night before the wedding, inadvertently out–staging the bride and the mother of the bride. Nobody looked happy in the wedding pictures. You must have known I was gay, but I could never tell, you never asked. My sister ended up divorcing and remarrying years later, after all.

I love you is a phrase we exchanged only once. Not when we celebrated your and my father's 50th wedding anniversary with a big bash, guests joining from all over California and Mexico. Not when I frantically rinsed dusty blond coloring off your hair in the shower after you came home from the hairdresser the night before the celebration with a new look that my father rejected, making you feel, at 71 years old, like an inadequate teenager—that's when you blessed me again.

You and I shared the same temperament. Like you, I can't tolerate incompetence or weakness in people, but I'm often shy about speaking up my mind. You too liked to tell others what to do, but didn't tell them how you felt. I inherited your facial features and your thick straight hair that somehow curls just so over my right temple. Whenever they see me nowadays, your sisters cry.

I love you is a phrase we exchanged only once, at your death bed more than six years ago. I think of you often. I talk to you sometimes. I ask you for guidance. I tell you I miss you. But I haven't told you *I love you* since you died.

You blessed me often, but *I love you* is a phrase we exchanged only once.

Runaway Orphan

DeLeon Peacock

It was 1969 and my brother John and I were living in what most people would call an orphanage. But, it was actually a chartered town, run by boys, located on the banks of the Altamaha River on the coast of South Georgia.

As an adult, looking back, it was a good place. As a footloose and fancy–free fourteen–year–old, maybe not so good. There were just too many rules. Like rules about when to go to bed and when to get up, when to take your bath and when to do your homework. I couldn't even walk on the grass without getting a summons to appear before the boy judge. In a kid's mind, too many rules and too much structure. Before arriving, I had been able to do whatever I wanted whenever. To be in a place that was structured on rules and discipline took some getting used to.

My brother John didn't like it there because he was a rebel and didn't bend easily. I remember John being in trouble of some sort the whole time we were there, and he had to spend a lot of time on the old hard tabby benches as punishment. I think my brother had the bench record just, under Stanly Griffis whose nickname was "Little Satan". The benches faced the campus chapel and I wonder if he ever heard god in an English Victorian accent saying "We are not amused."

I was a happy–go–lucky kind of boy, who never met a stranger. I'd be up in your lap before you even knew my name, allowing you to pet me like a lap dog. Why not, you might just take me home with you.

During Christmas at the orphanage some of the boys would get money from family. As soon as you got it you were required to give it to the house mother for safekeeping. On the Christmas of 1968 I gave my dollars to Ma Chambley, but John failed to turn his in.

My brother had a plan and as part of that plan he'd been taking clothes to school and stashing them in his gym locker. John was planning to run away.

On the Sunday before we were to restart school after our Christmas–New Year's vacation, John came to me,

"I'm leaving," he said quietly.

"Huh, what?" I stuttered. "Where are you going? Are you going to the Morgans'?"

The Morgans were a family who lived locally and had tried to adopt us. It had fallen through because our mother wouldn't allow it. John knew this and just decided he couldn't stay around any longer. He was broken.

"No. I'm running away. You can stay here with your friends or go, but I'm leaving."

It took me a minute to think. Did I want to leave my best friend Lynn whom I had a puppy–love affair with and planned to marry one day? Did I want to leave Ma Chambly who was finally giving in to my persistent brown–nosing? I had it good.

"You're my only brother and you're not leaving me here by myself. I'm going."

Looking down at me with a serous expression, he said, "You have to keep your mouth shut about it, understand? You can't go around telling your friends you're leaving and giving them a hug goodbye. You can't ever tell Lynn or Ma Chambly. If you tell anyone, I'll find out and beat the shit out of you." John was sixteen so he could talk like that.

Even though it half killed me I kept silent. I was so proud of myself for not saying a word to anyone. I was proud of myself because I had done it for my big brother.

John found a way to hook up with me later that day to tell me how things would go. We were to take the orphanage school bus to school as we always did, and after the bus left the school we were to hightail it to the Greyhound bus stop, where he would buy two tickets to Swainsboro, Ga., and we would live with our aunt Ollie.

It was time for another adventure and we did exactly as planned.

When we got to the bus stop, John stepped to the counter and confidently purchased the two tickets to Swainsboro, with the money he had kept from his Christmas mail, and put them in his pocket. We just knew that our Aunt Ollie loved us more than any other person on earth.

What we didn't know, was that Aunt Ollie had been the one responsible for sending us to Boys' Estate in the first place.

"I've got to go back to the school because I forgot my clothes," John whispered.

Before I could object, John was out the door. I was left standing there.

I looked around nervously, my mind spinning. I was so afraid that my palms were sweating and my heart felt as though it would pop out of my chest. I was fourteen years old and I felt like I was about to have a heart attack. My body became a big bundle of twisted up nerves and I wanted to find a hole to crawl into and hide.

In my mind, I saw police surrounding the building with guns drawn.

"Orphan boy, raise yo hands and come outa that there buildin'."

They would put me in handcuffs and haul me off to jail where I'd be thrown into a cell with Jack the Ripper.

I turned as the bus suddenly pulled up. But where was my big brother? I went out and stood next to the bus with no ticket. John came out a side door and we climbed onto the bus. We walked to the back and John reached over and patting me on the leg said,

"We're safe, little brother, because not even a State Trooper can stop a Greyhound."

Model Child

Chuka Susan Chesney

In a corner of the preschool, Lily was clipping a purple hair extension on a Barbie Cut and Color doll.

Her mother arrived. Lily grabbed the hair clip and hid it in her pocket.

They strolled down the road to the clothing store.

Lily wanted a jumper with a macaw on it, but Fifi bought her a sundress instead. The skirt twirled, but Lily didn't care. She knew the seams would scratch her underarms.

At the register, the saleslady brightened. "We're going to put on a fashion show!"

"Oh!" enthused Fifi. "How wonderful! Where?"

"The Castaway!" the saleslady squealed.

"Oh," Fifi replied flatly. They served cocktails at The Castaway.

Lily touched the hair clip. The saleslady didn't lose any of her enthusiasm.

"We're wondering if Lily would like to model?"

"Hah!" shrieked Lily. Then she looked down at her sandals.

"That would be lovely!" exclaimed Fifi. She could put up with a boozy restaurant for one afternoon.

The saleslady filled Fifi in on all the details. Lily would need to arrive with shampooed hair in an attractive style. Braids or a ponytail would be fine. The morning of the show, Fifi curled Lily's hair in hot rollers.

"It hurts to be beautiful," observed Fifi as she arranged Lily's ringlets.

Dale moussed his crew cut. Fifi slipped into a sarong, brother Toby sported a Hawaiian shirt, and sister Mae wore a kimono. Lily tucked the lucky clip in her sock.

Everyone piled into the jeep, and Dale drove to The Castaway.

"Are you here for the fashion show?" the hostess asked.

"Yes, my sister's going to be a model!" yelled Toby.

"Come this way. I'll show you where the Bridal Room is."

The saleslady strolled by.

"Oh, marvelous, there you are! Your curls looks so pretty, Lily!" she gushed.

Lily's chin started to wobble. Were her parents going to leave her here alone?

She pulled the hair clip out of her sock and snapped it to her undershirt.

"Lily," Dale said gently, "don't worry. You're going to try on lots of pretty outfits. Then you'll walk around the restaurant while we sit and watch!"

Lily dropped her father's hand. A lady grabbed her and unbuttoned her blouse. She looked back at the doorway, but her family had disappeared. The lady stretched a turtleneck over her head followed by a jumper. Her mother never let her wear turtlenecks—she said Lily's neck was too short. But this was a mock turtleneck with short sleeves. The lady replaced Lily's sandals with loafers. The kids lined up beside the doorway.

"Okay, kids," announced the saleslady. "I'm going out

there to get this party started. You do what these nice lady helpers say and remember to smile! You all look darling!" She left. The children heard her voice over the microphone.

A lady helper escorted a little girl toward the noise. The audience clapped and cheered. Next a boy in plaid shorts bolted toward the dining room. He looked like he was about to play a round of golf.

Lily tiptoed down the hall toward the tropical fountain. People were seated at tables in neon darkness.

"Here we have..." began the saleslady. Lily looked for her family. There was a bright flash. Her dad was crouched in front of her, holding his camera.

"No, Lily, ignore me," he whispered. "Say cheese!"

She looked past his shoulder and saw her mommy, Toby, and Mae in a booth, sipping guava juice. Everyone clapped. She patted the hair clip under her jumper and wafted through the misty restaurant. Soon she arrived back at the hallway.

"Hurry!" hissed the lady helper. She grabbed Lily's arm and yanked off her clothes, then wriggled her into a hibiscus−print romper. There was a locket around Lily's neck. The lady's fingers tucked it beneath her collar. She pushed Lily back in line and started on the next child. Lily paraded through the tables again. More clapping, then the lady snatched her from the hallway and wrestled another outfit onto her body. Ugghhh, this time it was one of those smocked dresses. The lady tied the sash into a bow and exchanged loafers for flats. She shoved Lily back in line.

The changing clothes/standing in line/walking through the tables routine happened over and over, as Lily modeled skirts, jumpers, dresses, raincoats, umbrellas, and ponchos. She beamed as she traipsed along, watching her family devour ham, pineapple, and yams, then rainbow sherbet and shortbread. But there were no refreshments in the Bridal Room. Not even a cracker or a cup of punch.

The show was over, and the family drove home. Everyone was tired. Fifi saw Lily eyeing the refrigerator.

"I'm hungry!" Lily said.

"How could you be hungry? Didn't you eat?"

"No, I was trying on clothes."

Fifi handed her a popsicle.

Lily told her dad she missed lunch. He made her a sandwich with too much mayonnaise. Lily had never eaten a ham and pineapple sandwich before.

A few days later, Fifi arrived at nursery school. Lily was painting Barbie's nails.

Fifi took Lily back to the children's store. The saleslady said Lily was one of the best models. She held up the macaw jumper on a puffy hanger.

"And," the saleslady added, "You get an umbrella!" It was a see-through, bubble-shaped umbrella with purple trim. When it rained, Lily could watch raindrops splashing over her head!

"Thank you!" the saleslady said. "You helped us on Saturday. As a reward you get all this for free!"

Lily wore the jumper the first day of kindergarten. She wore shorts underneath so she could swing on the bars and hang upside down like a spider monkey.

Nanna: When Justice and Mercy Kiss

Jennifer Rose

The pines at the back of the homestead form the boundaries of the safe, known world for my cousins, my brother and me. I am no older than six. My brother is fifteen months younger than me. One cousin is my age, one is a year older.

When I say the safe world is contained within the borders of the pines around the homestead, that's not strictly true. The homestead itself is a trap for the unwary. There are bees in the ceiling of the spare bedroom. Their corpses litter the Lino floor. The boxroom out the back off the sprawling verandah, where the laundry squats at one end, once displayed a live tiger snake hanging from one of the walls. (Nanna dispatched it with stoical efficiency all the while carrying my youngest brother tucked onto her hip.) The wood stove in the kitchen awaits the opportunity to burn young fingers if we get too close.

Outside, there are the geese, ever protective of their nests in the wormwood hedge, away from the house. And wherever the geese march in proud battalion, we children must not get too close. With their stern eyes and hard beaks, they are the very essence of fury.

Today we want to explore outside the pines.

"Stay away from the water tanks and the soak," admonishes Nanna. She's a short, stout woman with a crepey neck and a white widows peak. She *is* a widow, too.

We cannot obey her.

We clamber up the concrete sides of the water tank. It's half full and a haven for frogs and tadpoles. We don't even think about how we won't be able to climb up the five feet high walls if we fall in. We just want to watch the frogs swimming in the greenish water.

After we tire of the frogs we know where we'll go next: to the soak that's down the slope, away from the house, the pines and the water tanks sitting on the top of the hill. It's not really a hill, just a rise of sand that seems like a hill to six−year−olds. The soak is not very big. Maybe five metres in diameter. With reeds around it.

We play at the soak for a while, our feet sucking in the black mud as we explore its edges. We don't go into the water. We can't see how deep it is and we've been endlessly warned about how children drown in dams. And the soak is like a dam, isn't it? What we don't even think about is how tiger snakes like water, because frogs and other small edible creatures live there too. But none of us sees any snakes or frogs. Some tadpoles, maybe. But really, the soak is a bit boring for me and I want to go back to the house. So, we do.

Nanna is on the verandah waiting for us. She sees our wet trouser legs and skirt hems and our muddy feet: "I told you not to go to the soak," she says crossly.

Nanna takes each of us into the bathroom on the side verandah to wash down our legs and feet. Her face is stern, like the geese. Her hand administers a smack that sounds loud in that small room. I think a goose's peck would hurt more, but that's not the point.

I don't cry. I have received justice and I agree with her. Nanna does not hug or kiss us, but she is fair. I love her.

Helen of Troy

Larry Lefkowitz

Helen of Troy, possessor of "the face that launched a thousand ships," in truth possessed the tongue that launched a thousand ships. The reason that history has accorded her face the honor is not so much that she was beautiful (though she was admittedly that, perhaps the most beautiful nudnik in all history, even though there are those who favor Cleopatra), but that the Greeks put a higher premium on facial beauty than on nudging. (Discourse, or Rhetoric, had declined in Greek esteem ever since Demosthenes had espoused marbles in the mouth as an aid to effective speaking.)

First, Helen nudged Paris to take her to Troy (some say she urged one Troy to take her to Paris, but this is a canard). She was tired of the "ennui" of Sparta and Troy had a reputation as a metropolis with plenty of glitz. It was called "the Big Olive" for the same reason that New York (centuries later) was called "the Big Apple".

Then Helen nudged Troy to fight the Greeks instead of surrendering her. "Achilles has a weak heel," she nudged. "He and I once engaged in a mild flirtation during which I became intimately familiar with every part of his body. Of course, that was before I met you."

Then, after the victory was apparently achieved, Helen nudged Paris to take in the wooden horse. "Wood is in this year and I am betting on that horse to make our victory garden party the talk of the whole Aegean–Mediterranean."

In her twin set of memoirs (*Recollections of a Distaff Ship–Launcher* and *The Last Time I Saw Paris*), Helen claimed that she had actually nudged Paris to burn the horse, as it turned out on closer inspection to be decidedly non–avant–garde in design and was made of olive wood and not the mahogany which was in fashion – but that he refused, saying he needed it as a knight for a giant chess set he planned to construct on the forum.

It is difficult to judge the truth of much of the above, as Homer, who used Helen's memoirs as the basis for a large part of the *Iliad*, could not abide nudniks and Helen may have suffered accordingly image–wise in Homer's tale.

The Tattoo Girl

Bina Sarkar Ellias

She walked naked on the stage. Except for her scarlet high heels and the crimson shiny patent leather bag slung jauntily over her right shoulder. Except for the tattoos that clothed her from neck down, covering every square millimeter of creamy white skin. Her dark hair tumbled around her shoulders in untamed curls.

"I am Jewish," she began, "And my grandmother told me, in the *halakhah*, the ancient Jewish laws that date back to biblical times, women are equal to men." Her voice was as clear as the sparkling water of a mountain stream. "Yet, ironically, I cannot perform the commandments at the Orthodox Church. Nor can I claim my body as my own."

She walked around the circular stage, alert to the sound of her own words in the silence of the auditorium. "When I had my first period, I was slapped. Right across the face. 'This is a *Minhag*, an old Jewish tradition,' my mother had said. 'I do not know why we do it but it must be done.'

"Perhaps it is to warn a newly fertile girl that she must not indulge in stray sex outside wedlock, or to alert me to the duties of a good Jewish woman – to conceal the 'impure' blood in asylums of shame. Perhaps it is just to cage women 'in place'.

"I tell my mother and my grandmother that this act of slapping is barbaric and violates the norms of civilized existence.

144

And blood from our body is sacred. It defines the process of life itself. Why must we be ashamed of it?

"My grandmother had replied, 'Your body was shaped by god and belongs to god alone. You cannot defile it. Even a tattoo is forbidden.' Thus, I cannot claim my body as my own." She continued, "I must not taint my body with a tattoo, as to tattoo my body is to defile the work of god. The Torah, our rabbinic text, prohibits the Jewish burial of those with tattoos.

"My grandmother says my body is not my own... but I have claimed it..." And she walked on as if taking a stroll through Hyde Park, her protest inscribed all over that fragile body; wearing her nakedness like a grand designer dress. There was an epic quality to her demeanour. Like she was the central character in a Greek tragedy.

I was intrigued by the young woman. She was self-contained, in control of every movement of her body or twitch of her eyebrows. She talked of her dissent in even, measured tones revealing not a hint of stridency nor a shade of rhetoric. She narrated her story with ease, like talking to a friend at a corner café.

In fact, after the performance, I walked into the neighbourhood café. The Tattoo Girl sat in a dim corner. At the peril of appearing like a pushy tourist, I walked across and asked if I might join her. She smiled and pulled out a seat for me.

Shayna Shillony was built small. Smaller than she appeared on stage. She wore an army green jacket over a gypsy skirt and a large black hat that hid much of her face. Other than her face and hands, there was not a trace of exposed skin. Not a tattoo in sight. Shy, almost reticent, she stirred her coffee and looked like she longed to dive into the cup.

Was this the same self-assured woman, I wondered, as I complimented her on her performance and asked when she had first tattooed herself. "When I was sixteen," she said quietly, "I got the Star of David tattooed on my arm. My grandmother was beside herself and my mother did not speak with me for seven days."

"And your father?" I asked.

"My father left home twenty-four years ago, when I was two. I was told his name but never shown his photograph. I was told my father was an artist," she continued, surprising me with her willingness to talk. "My father was a bohemian artist. He had no anchor. He had drifted away from attachments, into his own spiritual world. We never heard from him. We are a family of three women; I was raised by my mother and grandmother – they're the strongest women I know; but deeply religious… and blinded by their faith. Much as I loved them, I longed to escape their limited lives, just as my father had."

How then had she mapped her own daring journey? I reflected and asked, "How did you find your bearings?"

Shayna smiled. "It was meant to be the way it was meant to be… I had joined drama school, where I met people whose minds were wide open to the sky and beyond. They had no fear. They had no fear, especially of the unknown. It was a learning curve… and I felt liberated.

"I also learned that life can be shaped the way you want it to be. Yet, one is not always the author of one's life. Some-times, at a random corner, the unexpected waits for you. I got my body tattooed while holidaying in Devon. My friends took me to this little place tucked away in a back alley.

"He was a kind and pleasant man, this tattoo artist. Tall, with wisps of silver in his beard and a deep sadness in his eyes.

His name was Ron and we talked of inane things, as he worked deftly, etching the Tree of Life on my body; not the diagrammatic form in the Kabbalah I've been familiar with, but from his own imagination, complete with birds and serpents inhabiting its branches and beautiful foliage twined around my arm all the way down to the wrist. It took many, many hours to cover my skin.

"Much later, I learned his full name... Ronald Shillony. It was surreal. I had found my father..." said Shayna, gazing straight into my eyes as she had gazed at the audience.

Paul Peterson

John Bost

"The snow fell softly all the night.
It made a blanket soft and white.
It covered houses, flowers and ground,
But did not make a single sound."
— Alice Wilkins

It was much like any other morning, until it wasn't.

I woke up bright and early, though actually it was still quite dark out 'cause the sun was not expected to rise until sometime after nine–thirty. But, that was no big surprise, since it was November first in Fairbanks, Alaska. After turning on the radio to hear the latest news, I brewed up a fresh hot pot of coffee to help start my day. While waiting for it percolate, I drank some leftover cold coffee. It seemed kind of like a cold shower in a cup — quite invigorating — sort of like the latest news some–times.

Next, as per usual, I reached into the kitchen cupboards for one of my favorite bowls. In one of these, I would pour cold cereal and milk. This I had done since I was very young, in Maine, using one of these same bowls. I now had the complete set of the six bowls I'd grown up with in my family. We'd shared many a meal in these cherished bowls. There might be *Cheerios* or *Rice Krispies* with milk in the morning, in bowls that later warmed tomato soup from *Campbell's* right out of a can. No doubt there'd be some saltine crackers and hot grilled cheese sandwiches, as well. Come dinnertime, for dessert, scoops of *Sealtest* ice cream were savored from those very same favorite bowls. There might be chocolate or vanilla ice cream with hot sauce, butterscotch or chocolate it often was. So now, cold cereal with milk in the morning is still the way to start each new day. I'd sometimes sprinkle sliced bananas over the top.

When they sprinkled and gently fell on my cereal this day, I was reminded of the falling snow that steadily fell outside my window. It softly sailed down, covering the ground and painting tree branches — the still and stately birch and nearby neighborly spruce. I couldn't help but watch the myriad snowflakes dancing in mid−air as they fell.

It was time, though, to get a move on. If I didn't hurry up, I would be late to meet my friend Tom Whelden for our regular morning walk. After putting the breakfast dishes in soapy water, I strolled down my hallway to brush my teeth and get dressed for the outdoors. I pulled on a pair of comfy corduroy slacks, a well−worn long sleeve chamois shirt, and soon sat down to slip on some thick wool socks. Then I was off to find my wool hat, gloves, and scarf. All that was left was my insulated boots and my trusty gray wool long overcoat. But, then I also dare not forget my umbrella, for it was sure still snowing quite steadily.

Before venturing out, I grabbed the morning paper that my paperboy had left behind my screen door. Folding it a couple of times, I then tucked it under my arm. Soon I saw Tom, with his little dog Melvin, heading my way down the lane. We walked a while, talking of this and that. There was a play Tom was in the midst of writing that he was eager to share and hear my thoughts on. The scene he currently was working on involved two characters lost in conversation. One character had some trouble he was anxious to untangle. I was intrigued because I sensed that Tom was experiencing some of his own troubles as well. There was something about the way he described this character and his situation that reminded me of Tom himself.

We stopped with Melvin by the roadside, while we continued to talk and watch the increasingly steady fall of snowflakes. I opened up my umbrella, held it up, and heard the flakes gently landing above my head. Looking over at Tom, I wondered why he was wearing his long camelhair coat, which his dad used to wear. It struck me as unusual, 'cause he usually only wore it on special occasions.

Then, seeing the three Kaplan kids building a snowman outside in their front yard briefly reminded me of how I loved building snowmen as a kid. But, suddenly Tom's dog barked, and strained on his leash. Looking up and out in the distance, through falling snow and misty ice fog, I couldn't believe what I saw. Tom and I both stood transfixed in wonder. Walking across the wide–open field, between two houses, was a small herd of snow elephants.

So determined in their stride, focused on their mission, they didn't notice us. Rudyard Kipling once wrote about an elephant with insatiable curiosity. I too, have that. My name is Paul Peterson, part–time private eye.

The elephants disappeared behind some houses and out of sight. I had read about snow elephants being seen briefly and on rare occasions in Canada, but never in Alaska. I told Tom what I'd learned from the eminent scholar, Quint Buchholz, in a prominent journal article. He wrote that these elephants are "even bigger than African elephants, and they have thick white fur – sort of like polar bears. They're very shy and they come out of the woods only in fierce blizzards. Even though they are so large, they move quietly and gracefully. Only very rarely can you see them pass by. And usually, before you've had a chance to look closely, they've already disappeared into the blowing snow."*

I wanted to solve this mystery, before I too disappeared.

*Buchholz, Quint (1997), *The Collector of Moments*, p. 6

My Dad, the Kidnapper

Tim Jarvis

There's no law or custom about how you should behave as a kidnap victim.

So, when I'd been kidnapped for the third time in the same week, I might not have been giving away all the behavioural signs. Laughing, for one, may have been a slight indication that I was less getting kidnapped – and more taking the piss.

You see my dad was deaf. Like total deaf. Like sing or shout as loud as you want kind of deaf. How did that affect me? Well, I played a little game of kidnap victim. Shouting for help out of the car window to anyone on the passing pavement. "Help!!!! This man is kidnapping me," "Call the Police!!" Funnily enough, no one believed me. Not one single person called the cops, not one single person came to help us. They either saw through the paper–thin charade, or maybe, just maybe, no one actually gave a fuck.

Aside from playing the victim of a heinous crime, I loved driving in the car with my dad for another reason. Being in the car did wonders for my music appreciation. I could play anything I wanted. Imagine seeing a man and his ten–year–old son, pulling into a car park with NWA or Guns N' Roses roaring out.

And they did, often.

*

I think around this time I was in my angry phase of music. So, it was all quiet, loud, quiet, loud type of songs. So, Nirvana played a huge part in this. Along with Alice In Chains, Soundgarden and various early punk bands or gangsta rap. Basically, anyone who was sticking it to the man. In this phase there was one voice and lyricist that soared above the clouds for me. Sure, Kurt had the anguish and frustration, Cornell had a voice that bent the very fabric of spacetime, but for me, it was Eddie Vedder. He had a voice that could rally the troops and soothe the injured at the same time. He could be with you in the trenches, in the dirt and grime, but he could also take you above it all.

My dad, blissfully unaware of the rock concert playing to a crowd of two (well, one really), would just sit there and drive. He was the doting father who came with a mobile jukebox as a great accessory.

One day, my dad and I volunteered to go to the super-market and pick up some food for the Sunday dinner. It wasn't alarming in the slightest that we were going a strange route there, as we'd often take the scenic route. What was particularly odd about this drive, was when my dad stopped the car outside a house. He tapped his watch and held five fingers in the air. His sign of telling me he would be five minutes. I gave my sign of a thumbs up. But he wasn't five minutes. Or ten minutes even. After twenty minutes had passed, I got out of the car and walked up the footpath to the house. I was more worried than anything else, I'd never seen this house before, didn't know who lived there, how they knew my dad – nothing. I admit, there was probably a lot of imagination going on from watching way too many shows about serial killers, basements and poodles. Because, you know, there's always a poodle involved. Any normal kid would simply knock on the door or shout for his dad. But me? Well, I didn't want to alert the killer. So stealth was more the modus operandi. Looking through the lounge window, there were no signs of bodies or struggles or even poodles. I Jackie Chan—ed it down the side of the house and poked my head in the kitchen window. Bingo. There was my dad. And his friend. A woman. Both naked. Both at it.

There's not much in the world I loved more than my dad. My mum taking the number one spot. But this was everything. This was like Luke finding out Darth was his poppa. This was Charlton Heston seeing the Statue of Liberty, this was ... this was shit. The worst part was when my dad and I locked eyes and he scurried to grab his jeans and shoes like he could hide the evidence and somehow reverse what I'd seen. I'd never forget that look. The look that he knew he'd lost both my respect and my trust.

They say in a nuclear disaster, the blast isn't even the worse part. Those who perish in the initial explosion are actually the lucky ones. The fallout, the oncoming hell is the real horror. And that's what it was like for me for the weeks and months that followed. Our home had become poisonous. I had to watch and suffer my dad play the good husband and father like a cheap daytime soap opera star. All scripted and forced. Whilst I watched my mother, unaware she had the victim role, carry on as normal. I couldn't tell her. I'd already watched virtue disappear in the eyes of my father. I couldn't handle the same in my mother. And weirdly it felt like it was none of my business.

It came to a head one night when I woke to the sound of her shouting. I presumed he was shouting back, only with signing. That was the eerie thing when my parents argued. I only ever heard one side. I hid my head under the pillow, put on my headphones and forced myself to sleep. My mum told me the next morning over breakfast and I played my own soap opera part. Storming into the lounge to buy enough time to rub my eyes until they look reddened with tears. She hugged me tightly and my fake tears turned real. Because I knew from then on, it would be just me, my mum and Eddie Vedder. And I may never be kidnapped again.

A Lesson Learnt
Rosemary, Aged Eight Years

Christine Law

The bicycle was in its usual place. Eight–year–old Rosemary was proud of her new cycle. She polished it regularly with chrome polish. The cycle was sky blue and red with a white leather saddle; a small wicker basket set off the chrome handlebars. The chrome shone brightly in the sunlight. The wheel guards in sky blue were always cleaned after use and the tyres checked and blown up with a small white cycle pump.

At first Rosemary rode her cycle with her mother Harriet through the woods and dales. Soon she would have the confidence to have the metal stabilisers removed from the rear of her cycle. In the village of Biggleswade everyone stopped to admire the smart cycle with the blue and red frame. Rosemary would ring the small chrome flower motif bell if she saw anyone she knew. She always rode her cycle on the pavement around the Harling estate. She never went to the shops unless she was accompanied by her parents.

It had been a surprise on her birthday, opening the shed door to find the cycle all shiny and new. "What, do you think?" her father Bill had remarked, removing the blindfold from her eyes. Rosemary had been speechless, hugging her father. It was her first proper grown up cycle.

She was very happy going shopping with her mother, carrying a newspaper or small items of grocery in the cycle basket. The cycle went faster than her old tricycle. Grandfather Horace had taken the tricycle down to his workshop to paint. When the tricycle dried, it would be sold at her grandfather's shop which sold cycles, car accessories and fishing tackle.

It was nice to ride her new cycle through the woods at weekends with her mum and dad. Squirrels appeared in the trees, while brown and gold leaves crunched under the cycle's wheels. Horse chestnuts gathered around the trees waiting to be picked. Everything in Rosemary's life was perfect. Soon the warm sunny days would be replaced by cooler weather. It was lovely to stand at the edge of the woods and see the fields and village spread out like a patchwork quilt below. She would often point out the familiar roads and landmarks to her parents. There was a fresh glow in Rosemary's cheeks. She enjoyed the warm sun on her back as she rode through the woods.

Rosemary had been riding her cycle for six months when her aunt Gloria and the cousins Wilf and Terry had come to stay with Grandfather Horace and Granny Elsie. Wilf was twelve with blond hair and brown eyes. Terry was slightly smaller at nine years of age with the same colour hair and eyes as his brother. It was the first time Rosemary had met her cousins who spoke with Cockney accents. Aunt Gloria had split up from Wilf and Terry's father Peter, and Granny and Grandfather had invited Gloria and the boys to stay for a short holiday.

There were games of hide and seek and fun fishing for tadpoles in the stream at Boscombe Woods. Life was full of new discoveries. Aunt Gloria, a small petite dark-haired woman with warm brown eyes, had taken them to visit a local farm, pointing out the pigs and cattle. Several times they had collected fresh eggs straight from the hens' nests, putting them into the cycle basket. Rosemary was pleased that she had her cousins to do interesting things with.

One day Terry asked if he could ride Rosemary's cycle.

"No, it's my cycle. You're too big for it. It's my birthday present."

Terry told Grandfather.

Grandfather said, "Give him the bike."

"No, you have other cycles at your shop, he can have one of those," said Rosemary, gripping the handles of her cycle.

"He doesn't want one of those, he wants that one."

"But it's my birthday cycle, it's a special present."

Terry rode the cycle when Aunt Gloria took Wilf, Terry and Rosemary out for short visits to the woods. Rosemary wondered if she would ever ride her cycle again, and would the cycle go with them when they went back to London?

Mum and Dad thought Rosemary had to learn to share her possessions with others, including the cycle.

One day they were going to the woods when Terry fell off the cycle, ripping his short trousers that matched his tweed jacket.

"He's ruined his suit," said Aunt Gloria.

Terry looked sheepish, getting up and mounting the cycle. Rosemary tried not to get upset at any damage to her cycle.

When Friday come, Aunt Gloria and the cousins had their suitcases packed. Grandfather ran Gloria and her sons to the railway station to catch an early train to London.

Rosemary was so glad to see her cycle standing by the wall outside Granny and Grandfather's house. As soon as Rosemary arrived back home, filling a bucket with hot soapy water, the cleaning process began.

Iris's Story

Jan McCarthy

I first noticed you when we were working side by side on the production line. Nothing exciting, was it? Just vacuum cleaner parts. While the other lads were rowdy and thought nothing of stealing a feel down an empty corridor, it being the sixties, you were quiet and respectful. Nothing much to look at, but that's not what counts, is it? *Henry doesn't fancy girls*, the lads would say, but I never believed it.

It was *me* had to ask *you* out in the end. Had to pick a moment when you were off–guard. A works' dance, while we were doing one of those where you change partners every time you go round. All the girls were grabbing a boy because there were more of us than you, so you got dragged in. Well, my heart was thumping in case someone else got to you first! But suddenly, there you were in front of me, blushing in your Sunday suit, with a nice white shirt and one of those Slim Jim ties all the lads were wearing.

Henry, I said, The Graduate*'s on at the Gaumont, I don't want to go on my own, will you go with me?* You were so flummoxed you said yes straightaway, amid beetroot blushes and treading on my toes. That was the only time you broke rhythm all those years, even when we were squashed into that mouldy bedsit we bust our backs to afford. You worked double shifts to get this house when Jim was born. I was so proud of

159

you and the boys. Jim left home, Nigel stayed. Just as well because we never saw that heart attack coming. By the time the doctor turned up, smelling of whisky, you were gone. It was Nigel held me together, or I'd have followed you any way I could.

You've been gone five years, and even Nigel has lost patience with me. Two years on, they tried to take me in hand, him and Rebecca, Jim and Virgil. Yes. Times have changed, love. *Mum*, they said, over Sunday lunch at Jim and Virgil's... You'd have hated it: vegan lasagne, sparkling water, fresh fruit salad... *Mum, it's time. We're coming over tomorrow to help you clear up and then we're going to decorate. You can go on a little holiday if you like, if you think it'll be too disruptive.*

The house still smells of him, I said, suddenly understanding myself after spending three years not. *It won't afterwards. I'll lock myself in. Don't come.*

Go on a little holiday. As if I would, all by myself.

They tried, the kids. I turned up the radio, shut myself in the kitchen. The last time the lino was cleaned, you did it and forgot to put suds in the bucket, so it was still sticky afterwards. I tore into you. Wish I hadn't now. You were too good, you see, so I took out my frustrations on you. You never said anything, ran your fingers through your hair, disappeared up the garden to check on your raspberries or whatever you were growing up the top end, past the pond you put in for the kids, which I've let go. Can't bear to see what no—you has done to outdoors. I know there's a dead squirrel in the waterbutt. Been a few months since I watched it slip off the edge. The frantic splashing. Can't look now.

Sometimes I walk barefoot on the kitchen floor, just to feel the stickiness and remember. You, not the squirrel. Your

160

clothes are still in the wardrobe, your pyjamas under your pillow. Your slippers smell, but I wear them anyway. Still got your toothbrush next to mine, the bar of soap with your whiskers stuck in it. I'm a mess too. Haven't been to the salon since our last wedding anniversary when you were still with me: Gaumont, fish and chips strolling home. We did it every year, in memory of our first date.

You kissed me, tasting of fish and vinegar, at my front door. Soft and shyly lingering. That kiss... I had to have you. Not ashamed to admit I chased you. Got you all worked up, a touch here, a touch there, you know how clever girls can be. Then I said, *Henry, it's about time you took me home to meet your parents,* and of course you agreed. Always a good lad.

Nigel and Rebecca push the odd note through the letterbox. They haven't given up, but they set me conditions, so they're stuck now. *We won't come round to visit till you tell us it's OK to clean the house,* they said. *It's not hygienic.*

Of course I talk to you all the time! Though our talks run differently now, don't they? I've learnt one lesson at least: no more nagging. I say, *Henry, would you be a darling and put some music on while I'm peeling the spuds?* Or *Henry love, draw the living-room curtains, would you?* Sometimes I still love myself and say *Ooh Henry, you always had such clever hands!* The kids would run a mile if they knew – even Jim and Virgil, who are so open-minded. Old ladies are supposed to behave nicely: knit for the kids and grandkids, grow sweet peas, have immaculate houses that smell nicely of lavender and baking.

Lily next door's coming round in a bit to take me to the spiritualist meeting. I haven't managed to contact you yet, but the chairman says it's only a matter of time and that you're smiling down and waiting patiently for me. You always preferred church, but the one that did your funeral – the one we went to at Christmas and Easter – didn't bother with me afterwards, so I never went back. The kids would go mad if I told them I go to the meetings. *Mum, Dad's been gone a long time. You need to move on. Life is for living.* They don't understand. There's no life without you.

Magna Mater, Sonny Claxton

Howard Brown

Drunk as he was when his car slammed into the bridge abutment, there were four moments from his life which Sonny Claxton recalled with perfect clarity as he lay dying beside the highway.

December, 1945 – He was five years old, almost six, yet still being bathed by his mother. He remembered splashing about with his floating toys in the old claw foot tub; the soothing feel of the warm water as she dipped it up in a cup and poured it over his shoulders; the silly songs she sang as she ran the bath cloth over his skin; and finally, the breathless moment when she held his tiny, flaccid member between her thumb and forefinger, and softly cooed: "Oh, yes, here's my little man."

September, 1957 – An autumn day when he'd slipped away after school and dressed out for football practice. Only to have his mother appear on the sidelines and shriek across the seemingly endless expanse of the playing field: "Sonny, you know good and well you're forbidden to play this game." Of trying to explain that he had permission from his father to try out for the team, and being cut off in mid–sentence by her shrieking pronouncement: "I don't care what that damned fool said. You get yourself over here, and I mean right now."

July, 1980 – The day his mother brought his lunch to the courthouse in a brown paper bag—never mind that he was in the middle of trying a case—and announced to the assembled courtroom: "Here's your lunch, Sonny. Make sure you chew your food well, and go to the bathroom when you're finished. Oh, and don't forget to wash your hands before you come back to court."

August, 1982 – Being arrested and thrown in jail for public intoxication, even though he was now County Attorney and normally the one charged with prosecuting people for such offenses. Waking up in a cell the next morning soaked in sweat, his head pounding, hoping maybe it was all just a bad dream, until the shouts and curses of the inmates down the way told him in no uncertain terms it was no dream at all. A little later that morning, hearing his mother bending the guard's ear as they came walking down the hall which led to his cell. Sitting on his bunk in his skivvies, smoking a cigarette he'd bummed from the janitor, and wondering which circle of hell he was about to enter. Then looking up and seeing her staring at him through the bars—the ridiculous wig she always wore just a little askew and her lipstick like something you'd see painted on the face of a clown—clearly poised to unload, but prefacing her diatribe with a single question: "Sonny, what in the world are you doing smoking?"

So, you can't help but wonder if in all the years that followed the grievous death of her fair–haired boy, Sonny's mother— Magna Mater he'd called her behind her back—ever paused to ponder the poet's words: "All men kill the thing they love."

164

Eve Survives the Genocide

Chris Hall

My crusted lashes were cemented together, so I smelt the horror before I saw it. Notwithstanding the gentle caress of flies crawling inside my nostrils, the stench of death overpowered my nasal passages and the heat of the sun scorched my face. The silence was deathly; the air motionless. No birds chirped and no wind wafted.

I detected a pressure crushing my chest but was incapable of raising my head to view the immovable object. Unruly hair matted with dry blood obscured my view so I could not determine the source. As far as I could tell, I had no obvious head wounds. My legs were also trapped. Reaching down I passed a hand over my thigh. It felt numb and at least double its normal size. The skin was taut, yet soft to touch.

Tilting my head to the side I peered down through one partially open eye to view the limb. It traversed my body at an unnatural angle. It must be broken. Perhaps that's why there was no sensation. Then I realised the leg was not mine. Not only that, in my peripheral vision I observed other random body parts strewn around me. A wave of repugnance overwhelmed me and I began to shake uncontrollably.

I was surrounded by human remains.

Once my vision adjusted to the light I could discern a nearby face whose glazed eyes stared unblinking in my direction. The gaping mouth exposed decayed teeth protruding past wizened lips that moved. Not a natural movement but generated by maggots writhing inside the mouth. The image blurred and faded for a few moments before I refocused on wild staring eyes crawling with flies. I gagged on bile before drifting back into unconsciousness.

My eyes opened spontaneously to the sound of distant conversation. It was dark now, but the moon shone with a soft luminous glow. I could do no more than lay motionless, listening to the voices approach. I held my breath until my diaphragm burned from fatigue and I was forced to let out a mournful sigh.

"I swear that one moved, it's still alive," one of them said. A figure loomed over me momentarily before a crushing blow slammed into my temple and re−invoked darkness.

I drifted in and out of consciousness with a tenuous grasp on reality. Noises nearby startled me. In a lucid moment I implored, "My God, why have you forsaken me?"

While I lay, abandoned and desolate, an angel appeared in my delirium and told me not to be afraid. "The Lord is with you. You have found favour with God."

Later I was roused by an entity gnawing at my arm, but could not reach far enough around to brush it off. There was no pain. It felt warm and soft. When I flinched, the creature retorted with a screech, dropping a piece of raw flesh it had picked out of a gaping arm wound. I remembered the day I discovered the dead carcass of Morgana, my pet goat, ravaged by fiendish crows. Again I was rattled with convulsions.

With steadfast determination I heaved myself upward with enough strength to thrust the restrictive body parts aside. I sat up to observe a plethora of crows, rats and dogs feasting on the necropolis of corpses around me.

What had my life become? I made a resolution that today would not be the final chapter of my memoir, if it was ever to be written. In fact, this moment would launch the next chapter of many that were yet to come.

Ernie's Miracle

Joanne Jagoda

It was the 1980s but I remember that afternoon so well. I was in the produce aisle of the Safeway when I ran into my dear friend, Ernie Hollander. I was expecting my usual bear hug and kiss on the cheek with maybe some playful teasing. Ernie, in his late fifties then, was a powerfully built man, quick to smile and flirt. He was bubbling over with excitement and had something important to tell me right then and there which could not wait.

Ernie and I worked closely together at our synagogue where I was part of a cadre of young volunteer leaders. He had been active there for many years, and he warmly welcomed me as part of the up and coming generation.

Ernie and his wife Anna had survived the Holocaust, though they had both lost most of their families. The family lived in a small town in what was then Czechoslovakia in the Carpathian mountains. His parents had eight children. Ernie had been sent to various labor camps, then to Auschwitz. He had assumed that only he and his brother Alex had survived. His own father was killed before his eyes. Anna, his wife, came from the same small town and had also experienced the horrors of the Holocaust.

They made their way separately to Palestine in 1946 and were to be reunited there through amazing coincidence. They fell in love and quickly decided to get married. On the eve of

Israel's statehood, the night the United Nations voted for partition, these hopeful teenagers who had already been through so much in their young lives, with just three dollars between them, married on a rooftop in Haifa with bullets whizzing all around. The wedding party, all twelve guests, were feted with one roll each, which Ernie had managed to hoard over a week from his bakery job. They shared their wedding night with the guests who could not leave because fierce fighting had broken out.

The young couple, hoping for a bright future for their infant daughter, moved to the States, first to Brooklyn but eventually to Oakland, California. Ernie owned a bakery in Oakland and in later years became a scrap metal dealer.

He was a legendary cook and with his wife whipped up fantastic community dinners to celebrate the Shabbat (Sabbath) and holidays. They opened their home to most of the synagogue membership at one time or another, epitomizing the words *gracious* and *hospitable*. However, the highlight of the dining experience was hearing their amazing stories of survival.

Though they had two children, they counted many more children as their own as they ran the youth group. The teens adored them and Ernie never failed to bake a huge sheet cake for the Bar and Bat Mitzvah celebrations of our synagogue children. Ernie posing with the kid and the cake appeared in countless family albums.

He felt deeply that the lessons of the Holocaust needed to be taught, and he shared his experiences at high schools, colleges and churches all around California. The audiences were spellbound by his stories and empowered by his example of resilience. He had hundreds of thank you letters from children and adults whom he had deeply touched.

169

When he got a call to appear on the 'Montel Williams
Show' to debate a revisionist historian, he did not want to go.
Ernie felt that even to appear on a program with a Holocaust
denier gave legitimacy to their absurd claims. However, some
community members he worked with on Holocaust projects
urged him to tell his story.

On the day he appeared on the TV program by chance –
but one might question whether it was really *chance* at all – a
young man from Yugoslavia living in Brooklyn was home from
work that particular day. He turned on the 'Montel Williams
Show', and when he saw and heard Ernie speaking, he was hit
by the striking resemblance in appearance and even voice to his
parents' neighbor, Zoltan Hollander. He could not get this
uncanny coincidence out of his head and called his old neighbor
in Yugoslavia.

Zoltan, his neighbor, was indeed a Holocaust survivor, but
assumed his entire family, parents, and seven brothers and sisters
had perished. Zoltan had rebuilt his life in Yugoslavia and had
two grown sons of his own. His wife had recently died. When
the young man heard Zoltan's story, he was convinced there
was a connection.

The young man persisted and got the Montel Williams
producer to call Ernie. Fate was set in motion. Anna took the
call from the producer. When Ernie came home from work,
Anna told him he had to sit down, afraid he could have a heart
attack. He just assumed something awful had happened. Anna
took his hand and gently told about the call from the show. He
shouted out loud. This news was beyond the pale of his wildest
dreams.

The next day, arrangements were made for him to call
Zoltan in Yugoslavia. When they spoke in the dialect of their

childhood, they quizzed each other back and forth with personal questions. They realized they were indeed brothers who had not seen each other for fifty years. Ernie had found his beloved younger brother known to him as "Heshie," whom he'd been certain was hanged in the concentration camp from a tree because people had seen it happen.

Yes... it had happened, but Heshie managed to get loose, fall between the trees, play dead and escape into the forest. He endured ten years of forced labor in Siberia, making his way to Yugoslavia where he became a printer.

The heartwarming reunion was held on the TV show. From there Heshie flew to California with his sons. Our community warmly welcomed them at the airport with signs and balloons. Heshie and his sons lived with Ernie and Anna for months. My life was changed forever by knowing Ernie and experiencing that miracles can happen.

Bob

Pat Bubul

Bob, the bartender, had registered the man earlier in the evening. Just another one of those coarse–grained relatives who likes to keep to himself. And to his scotch.

It was a fun wedding. No fights, everyone danced, and fives and tens furled like green roses in the tip jar. The tumbling crowd had thinned to one, and this old wolf was well past the level of moderate intoxication that everyone in town blind–eyed when it came to getting behind the wheel.

Bob walked the length of the bar to where the man sat—his head bent in a permanent bow to invisible royalty.

"Mind finishing up, sir?"

The man looked up, blinked hard, shook his head, and said, "Sure, sure."

Bob dashed away to relieve himself for the first time all evening. When he returned, the drunk man had fallen asleep, his glistening tumbler a nightlight beside him.

Bob tapped his shoulder, and the man slowly lifted his head. He had a gray–black beard, hair in a greasy ponytail, was maybe fifteen years older than Bob. The man looked from side to side, then at Bob, then straightened up and lifted his right hand as though preparing to give a sworn testimony.

Bob, who looked sharp all in black, appraised the unpleasant but not uncommon sight in this region of Pennsylvania: a guest dressed less for the formal celebration of a marriage than for deer hunting. A spark of irritation lit in him—a good night was getting tangled up in a drunk's disarray.

Breathe, Bob told himself.

"You have a ride home?"

The man reached into his pocket and pulled out a phone. He poked at it a few times; it emitted no light.

"Phone's dead," he muttered.

Bob would have let the man make a call with his phone, but he always left it home when he tended bar. And with everything online nowadays, Mike—Bob's brother-in-law and owner of this banquet hall where Bob occasionally tended bar—had stopped paying for the office line a few years back.

"I'll tell you what," Bob said. "Whereabouts you headed?"

"Mountaintop."

It was a 25-minute drive in the opposite direction, which was the last thing Bob wanted—the first being to hightail it home, where he'd kiss his sleeping children's cool foreheads and then slide under the covers into his wife's warmth. Fatigue was hitting Bob hard in the soft way that it does. It felt like weeks since the morning, when he cooked his entire family omelets and on his boys' plates arranged cut fruit into smiling faces: a cantaloupe crescent for a mouth, one green grape halved into two eyes, and a big red bulging strawberry as a nose.

But giving this man a ride would be the Christian thing to do.

"Can I give you a lift?"

The man's eyes brightened a little. He probably rarely received such an offer, Bob thought.

"That'd be mighty kind of you."

He and Bob shambled across the lot. The man wedged an unlit cigarette between his lips.

"I'm Bob. What's your name?"

"Frank."

"Good to meet you, Frank," Bob said, extending a hand.

They were walking six inches apart, but Frank, purblind and preoccupied digging for a light, missed Bob's hand entirely. Bob smiled to himself. Then Frank turned his blue bloodshot eyes and brightening cigarette toward him and said, "It's good to meet you, Bob." It was a good shake—firm grip with three hearty pumps.

Twenty minutes later, Frank was navigating Bob through a vast archipelago of mobile homes that Bob never knew existed, despite having lived fifteen miles away for forty years.

Frank raised a gnarled finger and said, "This one coming up on the left."

Bob pulled up to a scrape of lawn.

"It was very kind of you to give me a lift, Bob. I don't have anything to repay you with but this." Frank fetched from his pocket a dilapidated joint.

"You partake?"

Bob was surprised, and a little touched.

"Thanks so much, Frank. I do, but not tonight."

"It's yours then," Frank said as he lowered it into the cup holder between them.

"Thanks, Frank."

"Be well, Bob."

Frank patted Bob's shoulder with his left hand and turned to open the door with his right. Bob watched the stranger enter his home as the moonlight illuminated his hands dangling over the wheel. He fished a tissue from his pocket, wrapped it around the joint, and placed it in the glove compartment. He eased his right foot down and U-turned toward home.

Miss Grace Cossington Smith, OBE, AO

Patricia Unsworth

There seems to be no personality, it is long gone, laid to rest with her. Yet search her paintings and something creeps through, not only her life, but Grace herself. She is not just a name in the corner of a canvas.

Cossington was acquired, thrown in the middle. Her name was plain Miss Smith, Miss Grace Smith. *Cossington* was a professional touch, drawn down from her English heritage, an encouragement to accept the seriousness of her work.

Born in Sydney to English parents, her background was privileged, no necessity to work at anything other than her painting, no necessity to marry. Grace was well–educated, allowed to study under recognised artists and to spend further time travelling and studying.

At nineteen she and her elder sister sailed to England where she spent two years living with an aunt before travelling into Europe. Almost a latter–day Grand Tourer, but one who still studied her art both in England and Germany. It was during this time she was introduced to the post–impressionist movement, which was to influence her own style of modernism.

On her return to Sydney, Grace resumed classes with Antonio Dattilo–Rubbo, with whom she had previously studied drawing, but now she commenced painting. Rubbo had also become interested in the post–impressionists and it was in his studio Grace developed her art.

Her first picture to be exhibited, *The Sock Knitter*, painted in 1915, became recognised as the first post–impressionist work to be shown in Australia. It was this portrait which commenced the long–term exhibiting of her work and gained not only the recognition of her ability amongst her fellow artists but also their respect.

Greatly influenced by Cézanne, her technique developed with short, quick brushstrokes and unashamed use of colour. Her subjects, with relatively few exceptions, depicted the life she led. She painted portraits of her sisters, relaxed in their comfortable home. The picture acclaimed above, of her sister knitting socks for wartime soldiers and her brightly depicted work of reinforcements marching off to join the battlefront, give no feeling for the horror of war. The First World War was somewhere else. With her works relating to the Second World War there was a greater acknowledgement of the times, but she was still at home in Sydney.

Grace illustrated the visit of the Prince of Wales, painted beautifully attired people in a restaurant and produced pleasant views from around her home. This was her background, this was the Sydney she knew. She painted a series of the construction of the Sydney Harbour Bridge and a number of what could be termed religious scenes of church congregations. Here was more interest in her home city, but also an indication of her Anglican beliefs.

Although she visited England and Europe again, her life remained in Sydney. Her home and studio were the same for most of her ninety–two years. Her output was prolific, yet she only painted when she was moved to do so.

With time and age, Miss Smith limited her work to the narrow confines of her long–time home. But always there was the vividness of colour in the most ordinary subjects. *The Lacquer Room* glares with red chairs, green table tops and yellow flooring; the whole structure of the bridge is touched with pink and orange in *The Bridge in Curve;* and *Church Interior* has the woman in a pink coat in the foreground surrounded by walls and arches made light with orange and even more pink. Her later paintings are full of yellow walls, doors and fabrics, one entitled *Interior in Yellow,* and orange and pink again predominate the features in her self–portraits. This bright palate was part of her character and still true to her approach.

Born in the reign of one English queen and died during the reign of another, Grace Cossington Smith was a woman freed from the expected constraints of her time, but, in other respects, for the majority of her work, confined to Jane Austen's 'two inches of ivory'. She painted what she knew. Awards came her way, although she considered recognition of her work was given too late in life.

Perhaps one of the greatest acknowledgements of her art was the depiction of her painting *Bridge in Curve* on a 1996 postage stamp. But such accolades generally come to artists posthumously, as did this one.

I, Brian Gallagher

Ruth Z. Deming

Were you there at Holy Week at the Vatican?

Whether it was fate or the will of God, I, Brian Gallagher, a simple parish priest, was there.

"Obedient" am I. When I am reassigned, I may or may not like it, but off I go. Myself and my music.

From my hometown in Wheeling, West Virginia, in the USA, I was known for my saintly operatic voice.

As a child, our family loved singalongs: *Oh Susannah*, *Edelweiss*, *Fever*, as well as Christian hymns such as *How Great Thou Art*.

I was invited to perform on the radio program, Mountain Stage, not far from home.

Shocked as I was, I did this so the name of The Lord would be heard. Of the thousands of oratorios, cantatas, and operas I have learned over the years, I chose to sing a happy song.

When I opened my mouth, these words flowed out on Mountain Stage: "Your love is greater. Your love is stronger. Your love awakens me."

A popular song, for sure, but it had the audience in the small auditorium standing up and clapping along.

A few days after I returned to the rectory, a phone call arrived from Italy. In broken English, Sister Hyacinth said, "We would like—a for you to visit us at the Vatican. Bring—a your suitcase for you will stay a while."

The Sister said a ticket to Rome Airport would arrive in the mail.

That is how I, Brian Gallagher, arrived in the palatial quarters of the Vatican.

The magnificence made my head spin. Artwork by Michelangelo from the fifteenth century was on display. Since this was the seat of God and the Holy Trinity, workers polished every single statue, removing the accumulated soot, grime and dust.

I was given my own chambers, a comfortable bed with my own attached bathroom.

One of my joys was to sing in the shower, with the water cascading over my bald head. Special green soap was held in the soap dish.

Opening the package, I listened to every little crinkle.

Music to my ears.

As I was drying off with a luxurious white towel, there was a knock on the door outside my chambers.

Thrusting my towel aside, I put on a yellow silk bathrobe. All of this was given to me by the generosity of the Church.

A man my own height stood there.

When I opened the door, a smile beamed across his aged face.

"Brother!" he said, embracing me.

"It is Francis."

"Ah, your Holiness, I did not recognize you."

I spoke slowly as Spanish was his first language, but he learned English since the majority of his parishioners spoke English.

Here was the beloved face. Hazel eyes. Few wrinkles. And a mystical holiness exuding from his entire being.

He invited me to join him for lunch.

He had a map prepared so I could find him.

As I walked along the marble corridors, I heard lawn mowers outside. Every inch of ground – God's ground – is perfection, like God himself.

The two of us sat in a small dining room.

A nun offered us menus.

"Do not think, my friend, that we are taking advantage of women," he said. "Sister Elizabeth is an accomplished pianist and organist."

"What is that number you play all the time, Sister?" he asked.

"Bach's Toccata and Fugue," she answered, bowing her head.

Once, the Pontiff had played soccer in his native Argentina. After he became a priest, he became a "hands–on" priest like the other Catholic clergy in his country.

Over a dessert of tiramisu – rich vanilla custard layered with lady fingers – he said he wanted to hear me perform.

"I would be honored," I said, wiping my mouth with a linen napkin.

Standing up at the table, words sprang from my mouth, just as Athena sprang from the head of Zeus.

"Amen! – amen! – amen!" I sang slowly and with as much feeling as I could muster.

"Bravissimo!" cried the Pope. "It is *you* who shall lead the chorus. One of our several choruses, that is."

I bowed and kissed the pontiff's hand.

He smiled and said one of the sisters would arrange for a rehearsal. A new outfit would be selected. "Though not as beautiful as mine," he laughed.

After three rehearsals, we were ready for the performance on Easter Sunday, the holiest day for Christians.

Maestro Giovanni lifted up his baton, and a chorus of seventy–five began to sing.

From tiramisu to The Doxology by George Frederick Handel.

"Praise God from whom all blessings flow!" we sang with open mouths.

The men wore sparkling white shirts and black pants. I, as chief soloist, wore a long crimson robe with a white surplice bearing knitted crosses on it.

Earlier in the day, his Holiness gave his Easter sermon.

"Peace" was his topic. He named all the wars being fought around the globe. It made us ponder. And wonder, "When will the nations come together?"

And, I, Brian Gallagher, was now one of the bishops. My promotion arrived in the splendid building where Michelangelo and Raphael and hundreds of others painted their masterpieces.

How holy I feel when I wear the sacred robes.

The pageantry was simply extraordinary. They say many people convert to Catholicism because this is something you can see, something tangible to believe in.

Our Jewish brethren offer no such rituals. Passover, for example, is a household tradition. Families sit down together, wash their hands together, sup together and read from the Haggadah. The finale is to hide the afikomen – or matzoh – for the children.

Sister Hyacinth told me I could stay as long as I wanted.

Lying in my chambers, I thought of this amazing offer.

What no one knew, however, is that I wasn't sure if there was a God.

Could I hold my head high if I went back to West Virginia?

Shirl

Alex Reece Abbott

Sheep, I recall. People, no. No one else for miles. And I guess it's a weekday, because my dad wasn't around. Probably driving the monster JCBs over at the mine and dynamiting dense, ochre clay.

And I suppose my big sister was at school, learning all kinds of things, so she could come home, full of it. Weekdays, it's just me and my mother at home, all day.

I remember her perched on the sun−warmed concrete steps. I've lost the pattern of her capri pants ... paisley? Geometric? Maybe Pacific floral? Something on trend, for sure.

She's catching some early autumn rays in her cats−eye Polaroids, conquering another cryptic crossword. I suppose she must have been smoking. I suppose she thought it was glamourous. I can't remember whether she knew about the health warnings back then.

Every now and then, she would have recited a more difficult clue with witch−chant calm, a methodical rhythm, as though speaking the words vanquished their power. And she would have been punctuating her clue−war with "Ha!" and "Gotcha!" and announcing the answers to no−one in particular, probably knowing that all the while, she was infusing me with words.

Occasionally she would lower her newspaper to cast a vague eye over me playing on the path by the front door, free-range ... where is my cage, the jail-railed wooden playpen?

I make a break for the lawn, exploring on all fours. Bored by grass and lawn daisies, I scooch to the border garden, where the soil has baked into hard clumps. I rub a clod between my chubby palms and watch the dust drift away on the breeze. I vaguely recall a sense of delight at my new-found power.

Showy, candy-coloured pom-poms buzz my eyes. I suppose this is where my mischief meets curiosity. I snatch a stalk. Fang petals curl into fat, vibrant globes. I bite the soft, succulent flesh. My mouth puckers at the strange musky, sweet-sour, perfumed taste.

Spluttering, I spit it out. I am not Chinese. Or Japanese. So far, my knowledge does not encompass tea-making traditions in Asia. Or flavouring rice wine. Or steaming leaves for greens. Or adding flowers to enhance snake soup. I don't know about garnishing sashimi, or insecticides like pyrethrum.

I suppose my mother would have known how the blooms were used, known that they weren't nightshade deadly. That candy-coloured globe just looked good to me. I know about temptation.

My mother swoops from the top of the steps with a growl. I must have dropped the chomped remains of my prize on the path. Laughing, she wipes petals and drool from my chin with her ever-present linen hanky. I laugh too. Jesus, not my chrysanths, she says, probably rolling her eyes.

That tang stayed in my mouth – and my memory. Perhaps she read me a story to keep me occupied for a little while, before she went back to solving her crossword.

Laura's Triptych

Mike Lewis–Beck

One

In a stationary store in Turin, I chatted with the clerk about Italian pencils. We worried over the competition from German lead, and the poor wood coming from Asia. And, what, really, does 'Made in Italy' mean? Is the label just enough? "No," the clerk said, "the erasure must come from Italy, then it can say 'Made in Italy'." She went on: "You can't even buy a pencil made from one place, one country, anymore." It used to be that price matched quality but not anymore and it is the same with wine. She concluded: "Made things are not what they seem." Before I left, I read that her name tag said: "Laura."

Two

In Barcelona I bumped into Laura. I espied her, strolling Passeig de Gràcia, immediately recognizing her strawberry hair. We caught each other up, and she reported she now labored in a Belle Époque pharmacy in old Turin and was in Barcelona for a training course. This fit with what she had told me about the sun pills she took, two years ago. Laura remembered that, and my bad Italian, and accepted my invitation to gelato. How those sun pills changed my life.

Three

On Good Friday we met back in Turin and walked down a Via Roma, with the Procession for Christ. The people carried lit candles while the priests, creatures high above in black, with loudspeakers, broadcast the liturgy, the Acceptance of Jesus. Motorbikes and firecrackers shot amongst our columns, as we turned into a medieval churchyard, where rain splattered the bricks. A tall blonde with a mantilla spread out in front of us, swaying and praying, making tiny cross signs above her chin while she kissed a thumb. Penitent as they were, they made no mark on us, as we squeezed hands and blessed the rain. We were singing in the dark and wet, like the others—some with a script, some without, but we all resonated with the words, the story, the tune.

Uncle Rod Smith's Chair

Joy Mawby

Uncle Rod was dead, found slumped over his model 774 Camelback locomotive. And he had left me his big armchair.

I had last seen him a couple of months earlier. He had greeted me with, 'Come and see my Dopel O Gauge Terrier engine. Isn't she a beauty? I picked her up at the Crewe auction yesterday. I would have liked the British Pacific Class 7 or Britannia Class. It ran on two cylinders, you know, but the bidding went too high.'

By then, I had sunk into his scroll−armed chair and fixed an enthusiastic expression on my face. Come to think of it, it was then that I admired the armchair − just for something to say.

Well, now I was standing in my garage, wondering what on earth to do with the chair, dirt−encrusted as it was. Gingerly, I lifted out the seat cushion. Under it, among the dust and fluff, something glittered. Glad of my rubber gloves, I eased the filth away and pulled out a magnificent diamond earring. Astonished, I groped around the edges of the seat, pulling back rotten fabric, hoping to find the other. However, all that came to light was a torn and crumpled postcard of an anonymous and faded seaside place. It was addressed to Uncle Rod and post−marked 1976. The flamboyantly written message read,

'...*ish you were here, C. xxxxxxx*'

I stared at the earring and postcard and let my imagination fly.

In 1976, a woman – Carol, Caroline, Charlotte, Carlotta, yes, that was the name I would go for – Carlotta had wished my Uncle Rod to be with her by the sea. This beautiful woman, of Spanish blood, with raven hair and flashing dark eyes, wore long red, lace–edged dresses, high–heeled boots and diamond jewellery. She had been performing flamenco dancing in the end–of–pier show and, on her return, had sat provocatively on Uncle Rod's knee, kissed him passionately and lost one of her earrings down the side of his chair.

That evening, I phoned Tim, my brother, and arranged to meet him for a drink. 'I've got something to tell you about Uncle Rod,' I said.

'And I've got something to tell you,' was his mysterious reply. 'How about tomorrow evening?'

At the pub, I proudly lay my trophies on the table and expounded my Carlotta theory. When I had finished, he shook his head.

'You're on the wrong track. Do you know what I found in Uncle Rod's attic? A big trunk of women's clothes. Fancy corsets, French knickers, stockings, negligees, fabulous evening dresses, jewellery, stiletto shoes and – wait for it – three wigs, one black and two blond.'

I almost choked on my wine, but knew the explanation immediately. 'They were Carlotta's. She must have lived with Uncle Rod and then something happened to separate them.'

'Big lady, then,' Tim said. 'Size ten shoes and XL clothes. These were inside a book in the trunk.' He handed me an unused air ticket to Paris, dated 1977. 'The note was tucked inside the tickets.'

I recognised Carlotta's flowing script.

'*Dearest, do come to me. Things are so much easier here, C xxxxxx*'

'Poor Carlotta,' I said. 'He didn't sell up and go to her. She must have been heartbroken.'

'Oh come on!' Tim was exasperated with the romance of my thoughts. 'What do you think is meant by things being much easier in Paris? C isn't Carlotta, it's Colin, Christopher, Charles or some such. He and Uncle Rod were partners. Perhaps they liked to cross–dress together.'

My imagination kicked into overdrive. Carlotta disappeared and in stepped Uncle Rod, in a blond wig, ballgown, high–heeled shoes and pendulous diamond earrings. In my mind's eye, I could see him sitting at Crewe Station, writing down train numbers. I shook my head. No, I would not believe that. Carlotta returned.

We didn't speak for a moment. We were both painting our own pictures of Uncle Rod in the distant past. Then I remembered the Uncle Rod Smith I knew – the most boring man in the world and I started to laugh. My brother joined in as I gasped, 'Oh Tim, you know what's happened, don't you? Our Uncle Rod has taken his secret to Train Spotters' Heaven, and you and I will never know the truth.'

Lizzie Halliday

Jacqueline Doyle

Lizzie McNally Halliday was in her thirties when she was convicted of three counts of first–degree murder in 1894. Before her sentence was commuted, she had the distinction of being the first woman in the U.S. sentenced to die in the electric chair. She later murdered a hospital attendant at the Matteawan State Asylum for the Criminally Insane, where she died in 1918, at the age of 58.

I've heard the stories. One million Irish dead in the *Gorta Mó,* 'The Great Hunger'. The bloody British landowners exporting cattle and grain as potatoes rotted in the fields. Driving tenants from their cottages, setting their homes on fire, leaving families to wander the roads and die from disease and starvation. Calling it "the judgment of God on an indolent and un–self–reliant people." Two million of us run off to other countries between 1845 and 1855, never to return, millions more after that.

I was just a child when my family arrived in America. In 1867 there were still "No Irish Need Apply" signs in the shop windows, there was still sickness and poverty in the Irish neighborhoods. I've had to make my opportunities. My kinfolk on the other side were starving and dispossessed, but I've never wanted for food or a roof over my head. I was no beauty ("naturally ugly," one of my landlords told a reporter), but I

191

found six men would marry me. "All women are the same in the dark," one of them joked. There are some say I poisoned him, and I won't say I didn't. There are some say Irish girls in America are ripe for the plucking, and when I applied to be Paul Halliday's housekeeper I put on the brogue, pretended I was fresh off the boat, not here twenty—odd years already. And sure you're a fine man, I told him. When he offered to marry me to save himself the wages, I pretended I was grateful. How could he have imagined that an Irish girl might pluck him?

The doctors at Matteawan ask me questions but why should I tell them the truth? I don't owe anything to anyone but myself. Am I a "pyromaniac" if I set fires? I burnt down my shop in Philadelphia for the insurance. There's plenty of others done the same, all of them sane as I was. I remember Paul's son screaming in his locked room after I set the house on fire. I hated him, so slow, so aggravating, tetched in the head. I hated Paul too, his hungry stare, his rheumy eyes and old man's shuffle, how he fumbled with the ties on my nightgown in the dark. You wouldn't have to be crazy to kill a man like that, would you, or those two busybody neighbors come looking for him. I raved in the jail cell, I let them think I wanted to do away with myself, but the woman who pulled the trigger wanted to live. There's been times that rage has overcome me so I could barely breathe, but I've always wanted to live.

The seasons change. Sometimes I talk to a doctor. They say I have "conscious impulsive insanity" and suffer from "homicidal mania," and who am I to argue? I won't be leaving here in any case. I perform the same household tasks here that I did for Paul Halliday. I sweep. I wash dishes. I wash clothes. I used to sew. When Nellie Wickes thought she could leave her job at the hospital to study nursing, I stabbed her over and over

192

with sewing scissors until she was dead. Blood everywhere. What did I have to lose, stuck here for life? She was dearer to me than any of my husbands, but she didn't love me as I loved her. Why should she be free to leave when I was not?

Again I made the headlines. "Lizzie Halliday, Ex–Gypsy, Adds a Seventh Victim to her List." "Once a gypsy queen," they said in the *Logansport Pharos!* Seven victims! A gypsy queen! It was enough to make a cat laugh. There were drawings of me, my face contorted with rage, but no one saw Nellie Wickes up close the way I did. For years I've dreamed of her wide eyes and shocked stare, the blood dripping from my hands. I was shaking when they pulled me off her, with triumph or horror even I can't say. I couldn't help myself, that's all I know. Maybe I'm mad like they say. So much fury, and no remorse at all. I wouldn't do anything different, but I don't say that to the doctors. My sewing privileges were permanently suspended.

The seasons changed, and kept changing. So the years passed. Leaves fell in autumn, snow covered the hills in winter, buds appeared on the trees in spring, the garden produced bushels of vegetables every summer. I won't leave this place until they pack me into a wooden box and bury me in the Matteawan graveyard. There's numbers but no names on the graves here. My name will be lost to history. There's precious few who remember me even now. People remember Jack the Ripper who killed all those women (the sheriff in Monticello told reporters I'd done those murders too, old fool!), the other Lizzie who killed her parents and got away with it (you know her too, "Lizzie Borden took an axe / And gave her mother forty whacks"). Not Lizzie Halliday. Nelly Bly interviewed me, twice, long ago. No one remembers that. But I never wanted to be famous, just to live life on my own terms. "The Worst Woman on Earth" one of those newspaper reporters called me. Am I? There are those who say I'll burn in hellfire for my sins, but I set my own fires, thank you.

Steve Carr (A Memoir)

Steve Carr

It has been said that writers are made, not born. That has also been said about persons who are gay.

My father had been a coal miner in West Virginia just prior to relocating his family, a wife and four kids, to Northern Kentucky and then to Ohio where I was born in 1954. He left my mother seven weeks after I was born for another woman and disappearing and leaving us destitute. My mother had an eighth grade education, and with the task of raising five children she didn't have time to further her education or even find a job. During my entire childhood we lived in near-poverty conditions, fed, clothed and housed thanks to government assistance and with what little help my aunts and uncles and the Baptist Church we attended could provide.

I was an average kid, of average intelligence, with no particular talent other than the ability to write, which teachers at every level of school helped nurture. I always made friends easily and had many of them at school and in the neighborhoods we lived in. We moved around a lot depending on if my mother could pay the rent, or as one child after the other left home, decreasing the amount of living space that was needed. But at home I spent most of the time by myself, creating imaginary worlds when I was very young that I inhabited while I played, and escaping into old movies on late-night television when I was a teenager. Told by a high school teacher who knew my home situation that I should use my writing talent to further myself, I began pursuit of my career as a writer right after graduation.

It was 1972 and the war of Vietnam was beginning to wind down, although it wouldn't come to an end until a few years later. I joined the Army to become a military journalist so that I could see up close what war was like. Because I tested high on the military aptitude tests before enlisting, I was accepted into the joint military school that trained journalists, the Defense Information School. To my great disappointment after graduation I wasn't sent to Vietnam, but ended up with a cushy job at the District Recruiting Command in Jacksonville, Florida, and spent the next two and a half years writing articles for newspapers all over Florida about the soldiers returning home from combat, and dispensing Army recruiting propaganda in the form of news articles about the Army. The experience sharpened my writing skills, but grew tedious and mind–numbing. I also couldn't reconcile that I was supporting a war effort that I didn't believe in, joining most of the US population in turning against it.

After my Army stint I spent some time in university, hitchhiked up the east coast of the US heading for Nova Scotia, but was turned back by bad weather, and in a moment of boredom, enlisted in the Navy for four years. After training as a Hospital Corpsman and Psychiatric Technician, I taught in the Psychiatric Technician Program at Portsmouth Naval Hospital, training other Hospital Corpsmen how to provide care and support in an inpatient setting for young men with psychiatric disorders. I never spent even five minutes on a Navy ship the entire time.

Without realizing it I was following in the footsteps of my all-time favorite writer, W. Somerset Maugham, who also began his career with medical training, coupled with a natural talent for writing.

It was while I was in the Navy that I came out as gay. I was twenty-three and it was both the easiest personal choice I made and the most difficult, because it freed me from having to hide who I was, yet it meant there was a possibility I would spend the rest of my life being subjected to discrimination and scorn. I completed my enlistment in the Navy without a single day of trouble due to my sexual orientation.

After the Navy, I finished college, majoring in English / Theater and then spent the next 13 years working in non-profit health care development and management, mostly in rural communities, during which time several of my plays, written in my spare time, were produced in several states. I also traveled all over the United States and abroad, mindful there were places then, as there are now, in the United States and within the boundaries of entire countries, where being gay could get me hurt or murdered. In some ways being gay is like walking on a circus tightrope, requiring balance and a keen sense of awareness of the audience watching you as you take each step.

I gave up the steady income in health care to pursue my dream of writing / producing / directing my own plays and began a theatrical production company in Arizona.

I retired early and in June 2016 began writing short stories. Since then I've had over 400 short stories published internationally in over 275 different print and online magazines, literary journals and anthologies. Seven collections of my short stories have been published along with one novel and a guidebook for other writers on how to get short stories published. I've been nominated for the Pushcart Prize twice. In 2019, I was on the cover of a writer's magazine and dubbed "The King of Short Stories." In May of 2020 I learned that one of my flash fiction stories would be included in the Art + Pride Virtual Exhibit 2020 by the Harvey Milk Photo Center in San Francisco. A Harvey Milk quote is, "All young people, regardless of sexual orientation or identity, deserve a safe and supportive environment in which to achieve their full potential."

I'm now 65 and in my entire life the only two people who have shunned me for being gay were my mother and sister.

No one has shunned me for being a writer. Not yet, anyway.

Without a question I was born gay, but made into a writer.

Charles

Gertrude Walsh

Charles had a plan he failed to identify, and was gently railroaded into the life his mother decided for him. His academic ability led the handsome first—born son from a small town, successful family business, to a seminary many miles away. He studied, excelled and left. That was only after he escaped. Firstly, into a bottle, in misery at the life that had befallen him. The second escape was really an expulsion. In disgrace, he was forced to leave the priesthood for excessive drinking. Free at last, he travelled to London. Versed in French, Greek and Latin and with a sharp mind, he worked as a tutor and a journalist. He dated. He introduced his love to his cousins who loved him without dutiful requirements. They always knew the priesthood was not for him.

Eldest of six children, five lived, his baby sister died of whooping cough when he was eight years old. The large extended family of grandparents and grand—uncle all lived together as he grew. He carried the hope, the aspirations of more than just his parents. His grandfather and uncle liked a tipple, while his father, the women and siblings barely touched a drop. His mother, woman of integrity and standards, felt the observations of small town Ireland. He had seen his mother lose her baby, a brother and her mother in less than a decade. Then he was expelled from religious life. There was public shame, neighbours discussing in huddles and behind closed doors.

His time in London, he was 'Charlie' and happy it was the mid–1930s. Maybe too happy, too much fun and decadence. His younger brother was sent to find the Prodigal son. His mother had received a letter from a colleague of Charles saying it might be good if he went home. There was no fatted calf on his return, just shame, silence, stalled conversations when he entered a room. With averted eyes, his proud and proper mother stifled or suppressed her words. She prayed instead. Her insurance policy to the next life had been cancelled, the 'Spoiled Priest' was home. His past, in the Seminary, in London, his unspoken experiences were over.

'Charlie' returned to being Charles. He then led two lives. The life at home where his presence was an open sore to his parents, talked of in the community. The other life, was of his mind, with his cousins, friends. He was smart, engaging. He tutored and acted, broadcast on radio, researched and loved history. He was now the 'Go–To' for visiting Americans in search of long–lost relatives. Fastidious in detail, he scoured books and graveyard headstones, checked land titles and births. He told stories well. He endeavoured to welcome strangers and visitors, finding conversational points of commonality or advance research allowing him to share topics that put them at their ease. Funny, with a wicked humour, his name brought a smile to many who knew him.

At home, he was gentle with his parents in spite of their disappointment, that disappointment fading in time. He left the house to give space when his brother visited with his children. Some row, two strong minds and for decades they did not speak. It was not resolved before he died.

He travelled far and wide, loved race meetings and festivals. My sister, as she sipped a Guinness in a pub near his home, heard his smiling voice before she saw him. "Don't let your father see you in here." He didn't drink at that stage. In fact, he didn't the last 40 years of his life.

He had routines, took a morning walk, that town too small for him. Older, he had regrets, wrote to his cousin in America, that ten or so minutes was as much needed to walk the length of streets to the reach of country hedges. He tempered the comment: maybe the time with his parents was worth the return. He was fun with his nephews and nieces who visited. His mother, in dementia, worried for her own mother's lack of knitting wool. Charles told his young nephew to loudly tramp the wooden stairs, a pretence he was checking on the long dead woman. He expressed tenderness to parents whose beliefs robbed them of contentment. He laughed more than they. Never married, nor his younger brother. Shuffling, short small word sentences and familiar ways bound them all.

In our home were objects he had made, a child's chair, a slatted double bed. In his home were books, plays, typed historical documents and endless research. He left a legacy of stories spilling out four decades later from the mouths of those who knew him. He lived deeply in the community, alive with story—telling, music, drama, history, friends. He found a life where he was. I like an expression he shared with my cousin holidaying there as a child. As rain fell heavily on a dull summer afternoon, he grasped a book, heading up the stairs. "There's nothing to do on a rainy day but go to bed with Rabelais."

I was with him when he died. I nursed in that hospital. Away at a festival, I received a call and got the train to home. Two sisters and a brother had been with him but left for their evening meal. I reached the door of the ICU I often worked in. He was there, alone, in the first bed. My nursing pal was moving quietly, smoothly around the room. I sat with him, the monitor's bright green light showing steady, steady heart, beat, beat, beep, beep and he slept. It was calm and gentle. I didn't speak. I hardly knew him those last years, he didn't visit, my father didn't visit him. Not sure he knew I was present, but I was. And then his breathing eased some more, his heart too, and gently, calmly he slipped away. Over. 72 years old. My pal came to me and said, "We'll mind him now".

Charles was my uncle, born 1912 and died 1984. There are more stories but not possible to include in the word count of 1,000 words. He grew up in North Cork, the eldest children born subjects of the British Empire, the last two born in The Free State, as Ireland was called after Independence.

This part of North Cork had a history of emigration to America and Australia, and our family had a number who did so in the late 1880s and after. Many of our relatives returned on holiday to visit, as is evident in the Census Forms of 1901 and 1911, which was not something I expected. Charles was witness to a time of significant change in Ireland and globally and the family home was a hub of visitors and activity in part because of the business they ran but also the nature and engagement of the family in local life.

Sydelle Bender Brown

Iris N. Schwartz

At family gatherings Sydelle Bender Brown often slapped the dinner table for comedic or dramatic emphasis. My brother and I watched plates clatter as, pinkish red and sweaty, Sydelle held forth about relatives not present.

We needed to be especially vigilant, as one or both of us were called on to: "corroborate" a story, nod or laugh appreciatively or seize cups or bowls tumbling from her frequent table slams.

During a visit she commented maybe twenty times that she "felt bad" about "the coffee perking weak."

Sydelle gifted cousins, aunts, and uncles doggy bags, even though her fowl was singed and her roast beef garlicky but cooked to stringy submission.

Come three a.m. Sydelle would be sitting at the kitchen counter, lights ablaze, downing cherry vanilla ice cream by the sterling silver spoonful. Later that day I opened the half–gallon container to find all dark carmine fruit gouged out.

Add Another Sis, Mom

Michael Dioguardi

"You're not going to believe this, Mike, but I have another sister." It wasn't the call I expected, especially from my sixty−year−old mother. The next chapter in the already robust Jerry Springeresque drama that is my mom's side of the family, just got soupier. But it wasn't the first time my mom had said that to me. In fact, it was the *ninth*. That's right, my mom has one full−blood sister, and eight half−siblings. My goodness, did my grandparents get around! I found myself thinking, what does it mean to acquire an adult sibling in 2020?

"She's right outside Portland, Oregon. She's got two kids, Mike! And they're the same age as you and your brother!" It's strange how these things work. "She likes hiking too! If I could, I'd buy a plane ticket, right now!"

She didn't. She—like everyone else—was forced into quarantine with her take−off date to be determined. It wasn't my mom who had made the discovery though, but actually her half−sister, Shirley, who played detective. They met for the first time in 2011.

With the emergence of Facebook, Shirley was able to track down my mother and send out a message, "Hi, sorry to bother you, but I think I'm your sister." Phone numbers were exchanged, and Mom's hobbies shifted from tv and novels to chatting on the phone with a sister she'd never known.

Mom's a go-getter and always has been. She had to support Grandma growing up in Patterson, New Jersey. Grandma was epileptic and was fired from just about every job she tried, following her frequent seizures. Between government checks, Grandma's only income came from Mom's double shifts at McDonalds and the local bicycle store: working quick jobs and making quick pay. It came as no surprise when years later Mom became the first female motorcycle cop in her precinct. She had the ambition and the wheels to drive it.

It didn't make sense that her finger hovered above the mouse; she hesitated to click. I read the screen, *JFK to MOB*. The notion of meeting Shirley threw the brakes onto her wheels.

Mom had heard of Shirley before, but she could only remember the negative. I don't blame her; it was during the roughest patch of both their lives. In 1993, my aunt Elaine—the true-blood sister of my mom—took her own life. I was robbed of being a nephew while I was only eight months old. Later that year, my grandfather, who neither Mom nor my brother and I had ever met, also died. The relatives came out of the woodwork, albeit sporadically, and with a substantial amount of baggage. Mom sat down with her half-sister Lorene in a diner in Hackensack. Lorene, the daughter of Grandpa's second marriage, slid the photo album across the table to Mom, the daughter of Grandpa's fourth marriage. Lorene was the first to inform Mom about her several half-siblings, including her half-sister Shirley, the daughter of Grandpa's first marriage.

After perusing through the photos, seeing the face of the man—the father she'd never known—my mom was corrected by Lorene for saying "my dad" too much. Lorene went on to elaborate, claiming that he was "my daddy, not yours," and that

205

he only married Grandma because he felt bad for her. Mom stood up and left the diner, never to speak with her half–sister Lorene again.

I understood why Mom hesitated to click, buying that round–trip ticket from New York to Mobile. What if Shirley was a witch like Lorene?

Mom's wheels kept turning. My brother and I joined her on the trip too. Aunt Shirley and M'uncle David lived off the grid on the Alabama side of the panhandle. Shirley tended to the garden and raised chickens, while David hunted deer and pretty much anything else that had fur. My fondest memory of him was his handing me a sharpened spear to "stick the gators" as we hiked off into the bayou.

Shirley had been maintaining a complicated flowchart of their ancestry for over two decades, discovering that Mom was conceived before Grandma and Grandpa were even married. In 1960! It was practically unheard of. They divorced a year later: Grandma's first and only, and Grandpa's fourth.

The long–lost sisters have been best friends ever since.

When Shirley called Mom to tell her about Allison—their long–lost sister from Oregon—Mom was somehow unfazed and excited at the same time; Allison's story was different. She was adopted by a Scottish family who were right off the boat and raised in Bergen County. But she was Mom's half–sister on Grandma's side; the plot thickened once more. Turns out, Grandma slept with the greengrocer (not quite the milkman) but it didn't stop her from conceiving another daughter with Louie, the Italian stock boy. Allison always knew she was different, with her olive skin and green eyes, in contrast to her freckled and red–headed parents.

As per Grandma and Grandpa, I think Aunt Shirley put it best: "They were sluts, Mike." My perception has never been so subverted. But that's now an afterthought. As we transition out of quarantine, I bet my bottom dollar Mom's first move will be a round–trip ticket from JFK to PDX. And if that falls through, who knows? Maybe she'll hop on the Harley and get those wheels turning again. Maybe we can add a tenth sibling to the mix—call it even.

I haven't spoken to my new aunt on the phone yet, but I am eagerly awaiting the day I will. I lost one aunt but gained two more—and that's a damn–good feeling.

I lost my mother to cervical cancer – I'm not losing you

Zélia De Sousa

'I don't need one.'

'It's for your own good.'

'Trust me, there is nothing wrong. I feel fine.'

'That's because you keep up with the process. Prevention is better than cure.'

'Surely with today's technology, pain should not be an option?'

'Agree. But until a pain—free invention comes along, you just have to bear with it.'

'How are you feeling?'

'Not talking to you.'

'I'm truly sorry for putting you through this.'

Silence.

'It's been a while now, say something… please?'

'It's embarrassing having my husband sitting next to me, holding my hand while having a smear test.'

'Should I remind you how many appointments you have missed?'

She crosses her arms.

'Cervical cancer CAN happen to any woman regardless of their silly reasons as to why they don't need a test.'

'Like what?' she asks.

'Like I am the only man you have been with.'

He continues.

'My mother believed because my dad was her first and true love she didn't have to have a smear test... I lost her at a young age... A vagina is a vagina, it doesn't care what you look like, how many partners you have had or how sexual you are.'

'But –'

'Don't you want to see our child grow up, graduate, walk down the aisle and start a family of their own?'

'I am not going anywhere!'

'Good... Your next appointment is in three years. I trust you will be going? Break that promise... your father–in–law will be taking you. I'm quite happy having someone else looking at my wife's privates as opposed to having me stare at your gravestone.'

'Ouch!'

'Rather discomfort for five minutes than have cancer.'

Deborah at 46

Colleen Rich

We took two photos that night, one with the men, one without. The one without has endured far longer than those relationships did. We are all piled on the one sofa in Deb's townhouse, the first one, the one she shared with all those people. This was before selfies. Those days when you took photos with your camera and didn't know if you had anything until you got the film developed. We look good. We *all* look good. No one is blinking or facing the wrong direction. And everyone is happy, smiling, maybe a little sunburned.

Deb is making eggs benedict in the newly−renovated kitchen of her townhouse, the one she moved into after Jimmy took the transfer to Richmond, after his back surgery and the painkillers. Deb is poaching eggs, swirling the water around in the pan and then slipping the golden yolks into the whorls. I always thought Jimmy chose the painkillers over Deb, but I was wrong. There is a woman. There is *always* a woman.

I don't remember the latest photo Deb posts on Facebook. We are in a kitchen at a party. That's me, clearly, and I remember the shirt I have on, a gauzy periwinkle thing. All of my blouses were gauzy back then. Dan from high school is in the photo too. Dan in impossibly short shorts. I'm sure his kids had a huge laugh when they saw that post. He was always so good with cars. Still is. I remember the time he fixed Deb's

Chevy Nova right before a Jimmy Buffett concert. He fixed it right there in the townhouse parking lot and then we hit the road. We drove miles to that concert, to the next state. I couldn't do that now. Not even with an AAA card and a cell phone. That takes faith.

Deb's new kitchen has cherry cabinets and a forest green backsplash. The room is full of ferns and herbs and a pot of tiny shamrocks, all appearing happy to be back in their bay window home now that the construction is over. The refrigerator is decorated with photos of other people's kids, including mine. School pictures, holiday photo cards. *Wishing you Peace.* Deb and Jimmy never had kids. She had fertility issues. Jimmy, well, he just had issues. At first I thought that was a blessing. Now I know that it is not.

Every once in a while, someone will post the photo with the train. Mostly when we are missing Tracy. Tracy loved trains. When we were in town and would hear one, she would force us to stop and wait for it. The gates would come down, pinging, flashing red. Often we had to get out of the car and watch. We were always in Deb's Nova, wandering around at night, looking for a party, something to do. It will be 10 years soon. Tracy's girls are grown, in college. I took that photo in the fall of our senior year. It was overcast, cold, gray. The train is a brown blur behind them. Deb's wearing her puffy navy down vest and holding a cigarette. Tracy's hair is out of focus, blowing with the whoosh of the train.

Just One Story About Willy

Jonnie Guernsey

Willy has placed several bags containing his belongings on a chair, saving a space for me. As I approach, he breaks into a warm smile, reaches around the end of the table to move his things, and says, "There you go. I been waiting for you."

Willy and I have been friends for several years. We're exactly the same age, born two months apart. His dark skin is hardly wrinkled, except for the lines around his eyes, laugh lines, worry lines. His Green Bay Packers knit hat is pulled low over his gray hair, and a scarf is wrapped tightly just below his beard.

I set my tray on the table and sit across from him. "Hey, want my cookies? I got them for you." I know Willy loves his sweets.

"Yeah, I'll take those." He pockets the cookies and throws me some adoration. "You sure you don't want to marry me?"

We laugh at this running joke. Only sometimes, Willy is not kidding.

He studies me for half a minute, eyes moist. "Where've you been? You haven't been here in a long time."

"Willy, I was here last week Monday. This is Wednesday, so I saw you days ago."

"Like I said," he repeats, "I haven't seen you in a long time." There he is again, sending me that beatific gaze. Willy oozes love, like he's sent from heaven.

I imagine that on the streets, your days are measured in minutes, concentrating on making it through this next hour, then the day, then the night, bit by bit, moment by moment. The people who live like this tell me that it takes a lot of time to be poor. Everything takes effort. Nine days, to them, is a long time.

"Sorry, Willy. I come every week – just not always on the same day."

"Well, I'm here every day." He chuckles. "You'll always find me here." He points his fork in my direction, eyes crinkling with affection. "I watch for you every day."

"And I look for you every time I come." Sometimes Willy isn't there when I hang out at the meal program. St. Ben's doesn't allow him to come in when he's really drunk. He gets belligerent.

"Oooh!" Willy scrunches up his face like something just bit him. "Let me tell you, some strange things been happening."

"Bad things? Are you okay?"

Still wincing, he says, "Yeah. I'm okay. But don't you know, it's been *hard.*" The last word is elongated, punctuated by his upper body rocking forward, and another, "Ooooh!"

"What happened?"

"Well, I fell asleep on the bus. The driver shakes me and tells me I got to get off. I was way out on Highway 100 and Greenfield."

"Couldn't he just let you ride back downtown?"

Willy shrugs. "I asked him, 'How'm I gonna get back?' Driver said it was the end of the line." He grips the edge of the table. "Don't you know, it was cold. One of them *real* cold days when the wind chill was so harsh last week. I started walking. I didn't know *what* I was gonna do."

"Were you riding the bus to stay warm?"

"Yeah." He lets go a rueful laugh. "But that only works if you don't fall asleep."

Something doesn't add up. In the dead of winter, most drivers will give a person a transfer, not leave them stranded. Before I can interject, he continues his story.

"So I'm walking on that busy street, cold as can be — shivering so bad, and it's getting dark." He glances around, lowers his voice and leans in. "I started going up to buildings and trying the doors, seein' if they was locked."

I inhale a slow breath, say nothing.

He holds my gaze. "I know it's wrong, doin' like that, but I thought, 'I'm gonna die right here tonight if I don't get out of this cold.' I asked God to save me." He pauses, mops up the tears brimming in his eyes with a paper napkin. "After while, I found a back door in an apartment building that wasn't locked. So I—" He mimes opening a door and peering in. "Nobody was around. I slipped downstairs quiet as I could and hid myself in the basement by the furnace. I fell asleep right there on the floor. But in the morning, I heard *clomp, clomp, clomp*." He whispers, "Somebody was coming down the stairs!"

I gasp and cover my mouth. The suspense is too much. I'm wondering what I would do if I found someone sleeping in my basement. And what I would do if I were in Willy's shoes to survive a cold night.

"When he found me, I stood up—" Willy raises his hands like a person stopped by the police. "And I told him, 'Sir, I know I'm not supposed to be here. I didn't mean no harm. I

214

was afraid I was gonna freeze to death.'" The rapturous expression returns to his face. "And do you know what that man did?"

Speechless, I shake my head, no.

Willy leans back. "He told me, 'That's all right. I'm glad you're okay.' He wasn't even mad at me or nothin'. I was so *grateful.* So grateful."

I know the warming room will be open at St. Ben's, since the temperature is only twelve degrees. "Maybe you should just stay here tonight." I don't like to think of him going back to the parking garage under the courthouse where he often stays. Willy doesn't like the homeless shelters. Too many rules for him.

He pulls his flirty face, eyes bright again. "You gonna stay with me?"

Trisha Ridinger McKee

Trisha McKee

I hide under my covers as the screaming intensifies. As the crashing and booming continue through the night. Any minute my mother or her boyfriend–of–the–moment can storm into my room and spread this rage, make me the target. It happens often.

I am too young to put up much of a fight. I am too young to escape to a friend's. But suddenly, I hear a voice tell me, "Close your eyes, and imagine a family you want. Create another world."

So I do just that. I close my eyes and imagine people who love me and do not harm me. I imagine no rage, no physical harm, no emotional trauma. Each night, I continue this world, adding on to the story.

When I am old enough to write, I create these stories on paper. It is my escape. It is my saving grace. The dysfunctional home life continues. The toxicity drips through the days, but I focus on writing and believing in better. I work hard in school and earn a full writing scholarship.

Life has other plans. I get sidetracked. Things happen, and I drop out of college. Twice. I have a broken engagement, low self–esteem, and no direction. But I keep writing. I am always writing.

I meet a man and move in with him the first week of dating. The first week. I did not marry the man I had known

216

for four years, but I move in with this guy the first week. Everyone tells me I'm making a mistake. He has a history. A broken marriage. A son. But I sense something past all of that. I see him.

We get pregnant almost right away. Things happen faster than a tornado, and it is all I can do to keep control of my life. But in my writing, I'm always in control. So I write.

My daughter is born during a snowy February day at the start of the new century. I am terrified of being a mother. What if I'm like my own mother? What if something suddenly clicks, and I'm that monster?

But it does not happen. I fill the maternal role naturally, if not traditionally. We are close from day one. She is the part of my heart that has been missing. She is what I never had growing up. This is my childhood revised.

And I write.

The man I knew a week is now my husband, and when our daughter is two years old, he encourages me to return to college. I stick with it this time, piling on classes so I can graduate early, since we need my income sooner rather than later.

Obtaining my bachelor's degree in English does something. It gives me that boost I need in my confidence. I land my first office job. I let go of the last attachment remaining between me and my maternal family. I let go of the trauma my mother has put me through all my life. There is nothing keeping me tied to her now. I know my worth. And years later, when my mother is dying, I visit her and tell her goodbye. I don't wish the suffering on her. I simply wish peace. As I did for the child I was all those years ago.

And I keep writing.

I stumble a few times through the years. Some setbacks in my career. When my daughter is twelve, I am laid off. It is a blessing in disguise. I start paying attention to my daughter's online activities. I ground her for a month. I realize she is back to the same behaviors. I take all electronics away for a year. One year. No phone. No laptop. Nothing. We spend quality time together. We strengthen our bond. She straightens her path.

I land a great job at Penn State University. Things seem to be falling into place. My daughter is preparing for college. And yet... something is missing.

The year I turn 43, April 2019, I step out of my comfort zone. I shed the last of my insecurities. I send my writing out. I let go of my security blanket, and I send it off to share with others. I face whatever may happen, although I still tremble at the thought of ridicule.

And now we are here. Today. I have had my work appear in over sixty publications. I have had my first novel published. I am still married to the man I knew for a week. We are best friends as well as lovers. He is my biggest support.

My daughter is my closest confidante. She will be a junior in college. She wrote her admission essay on her year without technology. Although I always have that dream of my daughter following in my writer footsteps, she is more of a painter, as skilled with a paintbrush as I am with a pen. Our home is happy, no toxicity within the walls of this house.

I still write. It is no longer a necessity to survive. But it is a part of me. It is my happy place. I am grateful for the stories I weave. They had saved me once upon a time. During that dark start.

Ryan

David Butler

Everything changes. The city. The faces. Even the bus route. The one thing that hasn't changed is the mounting apprehension as he approaches the housing estate.

Everything is pretty much where it should be, the bus-shelters, the mutilated trees. But the dimensions are off. As though he's walking through a simulacrum of the suburb. *Macari's* chipper is still there, and the off-licence, though the bookies is part of a franchise now and the *Cut Above* hair salon is boarded up. Was the carpark really so small that a skip takes up a full third of it?

His gut undergoes a queasy somersault as he pushes through the carpark. Halfway along Oakwood Drive will be the stunted passageway that leads into the old estate. The shortcut. That's where they used to wait for him. You could walk on, take the long way round. But then they'd jeer, maybe follow you along the street, pushing. Mocking.

Or they'd cut across the green and be waiting by the main entrance.

So, at the beginning of Oakwood Drive, Ryan stops. He pulls out an inhaler, aspirates the clammy anxiety filming his mouth. Why has he come out here? What's it supposed to achieve, anyway? He hears a click–clack of high–heels. Across the road, an African woman pushing a pram flashes eyes at him as though asking if he's alright. Ryan smiles weakly, holds up a hand, *just a bit dizzy is all.*

Why *has* he come out here? Chances are, Janine wouldn't have been bothered either way. She wouldn't even have to know whether he came out or not. But from the moment she'd remarked, as though casually, that the old family home was up on myhome.ie, he'd known that this day, this visit, was inevitable. The house in which their mother died, all those years ago. Laying ghosts, isn't that the way she'd put it?

Ryan checks his watch. He's early. The estate agent won't be there to meet him before a quarter past. But he can't very well stand here like a vagrant watching traffic go by.

It's been more than fifteen years since he's walked this footpath. A year after their mother died, they'd moved to Bray. New school. New start. Prozac, to keep the anxiety down. Janine stepped in to fill their mother's shoes, though she was barely fourteen.

All the same, with each step, dread churns in his gut, heavy as wet cement. Which is crazy. For Christ's sake, he's twenty-five years old!

Seeing a group of youngsters up ahead, Ryan walks faster. He frowns, to look purposeful. His nerves are jumpy as a bag of cats. All his life, his body has betrayed him, emotions sluicing about like unbaled water in a boat. But already, beyond the youngsters, he can see the mouth of the stunted passageway.

The concrete bollards are pretty much as he remembers them, two tusks in a gaping maw. But what terrors can the passage hold for him now, with its stink of piss and snarls of graffiti? It looks smaller, shorter. Thirty paces will see him through it.

The worst of them was Damo Kelly. He was two years above them in school. What the hell was he doing, lording it over a gang of nine-year-olds? Because the worst of it was, the ribbing continued, even inside the classroom. The casual kicks, the Chinese burns. He'd done nothing whatsoever to them, but Hickey, Roche and O'Sullivan had it in for him. Damo Kelly's sidekicks. They'd take a book, or a flask, or even his inhaler, and throw it from one to another just out of his reach.

Ryan emerges from the passageway unscathed. Now the street where they lived opens before him, curving about the green. And there is 26, a *For Sale* sign by the gate. Would revisiting the house really lay all those ghosts, as Janine seemed to think?

Ryan doesn't see how it could.

A month into fifth class, their father took them aside, told them about the diagnosis. Liver cancer. She'd been given three to four weeks, no more. All that month, at school assembly, the principal had the whole school offer up a prayer for her, not that she'd recover, but that she'd have a peaceful passing. That's how Ms ní Bhroin termed it. A peaceful passing.

Ryan stands by the gate of 11, looks across the road at 26. The garden looks manicured now, smaller somehow, though still overshadowed by next-door's birch. The door is buttercup yellow, now. But the upstairs windows watch him with the same inscrutable stare as when he lived here. Will he really stand inside, again? Enter the bedroom where his mother lay dying, hear again the flippant whir of the morphine-pump?

All that month, Roche and Hickey and O'Sullivan gave him a wide berth. Where previously he'd been ignored by the class, there was something approaching reverence in the new attitude toward him. Damo Kelly's gang no longer waited for him in the mouth of the passageway. And the deference continued, too, even after the funeral. All that year, in fact. Then the following summer, they'd moved to Bray.

A red Clio pulls up outside 26. A woman in a tailored suit steps out, clipboard under her arm. She shields her eyes and peers over at him. 'Gavan Ryan?' she calls, with a humorous grimace.

Ryan detaches himself from the pillar. 'No,' he calls back. 'No, sorry.'

He makes back toward Oakland Drive, his heart skittering about like a bird in a cage. Because that was one thing he's never told Janine. That he never can tell Janine. All that last year they'd lived here, after their mother's wake, Ryan felt as though a great weight had been lifted from him. He no longer made his way to school and back in mortal dread.

For the first and only time in his life, Ryan had almost been a celebrity.

We_a

David Strickland

$We_{a,\alpha}$ joined as most do, with good intentions and unspoken pressure. Two humans reaching out in the dark, our biology and society signaling that now was the time to begin our genetic legacy. Others suggested that even with extended lifespans, forty–five years was a long time to exist outside of the Dichotomy. Our forebears had certainly not waited as long. $We_{a,\alpha}$, however, had been content to seek solace in ourselves until then. Not that $we_{a,\alpha}$ had avoided coupling with others, but they were transient bonds with no chance to face a decade without crumbling, much less the century or more often observed in the Dichotomy. A successful dyad and the resulting legacy it must produce – $we_{a,\alpha}$ had both felt at the time – would require something more than mere feeling.

$We_{a,\alpha}$ courted for five years, living together as a dyad in all but title. The joys were normal, as were the hardships. $We_{a,\alpha}$ observed others undergo dissolution, spoke frankly with ourselves as we tried to divine their cause. $We_{a,\alpha}$ argued – infrequently – and sought to solve our dissonant viewpoints by compromise. Introspection was a normal aspect of our life, a tool with which to dissect our thoughts and feelings. With unearned optimism $we_{a,\alpha}$ thought ourselves deserving of dyad status, especially considering the advanced age at which $we_{a,\alpha}$ would be joining compared to our peers. Yet despite our preparations $we_{a,\alpha}$ did not fully understand the commitment $we_{a,\alpha}$ had made to one another as $we_{a,\alpha}$ recited the vows, swapped segments of our neural discs, and became one.

Six months after the ceremony were all it took to learn that a genetic legacy would be impossible for our dyad to produce. $We_{a,\alpha}$ mourned this loss and in doing so poured ourselves into our work. We_a were an expert in somatic embryogenesis: conjuring whole plants from single somatic cells grown in culture. We_α were also an entrepreneur, less interested in the particulars of the auxin and gibberellin ratios we_a tinkered with and more in the final application of our work to the benefit of the Dichotomy. An admittedly qualitative skillset, but we_a did not seem to mind the inherent risk to our livelihood. Together $we_{a,\alpha}$ made an excellent team and during the next three decades operated a business propagating rootstock. The populations of New York, Michigan, and Liberated Ontario were expanding dramatically due to their rare proximity to fresh water; our dyadic interaction produced millions of apple, cherry, and grape propagules to meet the demand for a continent inexorably losing arable land to climate change.

During the holidays $we_{a,\alpha}$ would make the obligatory journey west to visit with family and hear the same obligatory statements from them regarding our childlessness. Their genetic legacy was dependent on our own. To escape probing questions, $we_{a,\alpha}$ would go for walks amidst the decaying wood of Oregon's long–defunct national parks, gazing upon the petrified trunks of leafless behemoths that $we_{a,\alpha}$ remembered so differently from our youth. $We_{a,\alpha}$ reflected upon their loss, mourning for the generations that would never experience their humbling presence, including our own. Yet while walking those desolate paths, we$_{a,\alpha}$ had a thought that sang in our twinned soul. We$_{a,\alpha}$ could revive the redwoods.

The task was arduous, a challenge like no other that we$_a$ had yet faced. The redwoods had vanished from the continent by drought, fire, and human machination. A callus was obtained from germplasm stored in far–off New Zealand, where a singular grove still grew. We$_a$ coaxed viable meristematic tissue from it with a cocktail of plant hormones: the precursor to our goal. Four decades passed, and in the interim, as we$_a$ worked, we$_\alpha$ also set in motion the necessities with the Dichotomy required for our unique legacy to succeed.

The rootstock business suffered as we$_a$ poured more of ourselves into the redwoods – we$_{a,\alpha}$ gradually lost our edge to competitors. During those lean years we$_\alpha$ worked odd jobs to keep food on the table and power to the generators of the tissue culture lab. We$_{a,\alpha}$ fought, more than we would like to admit, and some lonely nights we$_{a,\alpha}$ reflected on the dissolution pacts made by dyads decades ago. Sometimes only our shared vision safeguarded our union, although we$_\alpha$ would probably suggest stubbornness too. We$_{a,\alpha}$ felt that our union was a choice, not a destiny. Each day and decade were earned through sacrifice and joint decisions. We$_{a,\alpha}$ were obligated to foster our personal growth for our continual betterment, no matter the present circumstances.

We$_a$ sit here now amidst what will be the first national park on the west coast in two centuries. The results of our toil are spread upon the mountainside for inspection: thousands of trees brought from our Michigan nurseries across this fractured country and replanted in Oregonian soil. The light of its first sunrise bathes the grove of fledgling redwoods, promoting growth to summon their leafy crowns skyward. It will be many centuries before they join their ancestors. In the distance, we_a note the gleaming metal pipes of the new desalinization plant that will feed transformed sea water to this barren landscape.

We_a sit amongst these trees alone. The time of our dyad is over, a purposeless accident having riven ourselves three years ago. We_α will never sit here to observe the fruits of our legacy, and the smiles of delight it brings to others in the Dichotomy.

Our breath shudders with unbidden grief, our insides carrying the wound of absence like a penance. It will heal, in time. Another century will pass and we_a will have difficulty recalling the details of our time together. When we_a journey west, we_a will rely on this redwood grove for those memories.

But for now, we_a are alone.

I am alone.

Billy

Elaine Barnard

Billy keeps talking. I keep cycling wishing he'd stop, let me finish my gym routine. I have to finish my routine. If I don't finish I have a sort of hole in my day, in my head, in my heart. I depend on routine for my sanity. Some might say my happiness. But happiness is a questionable term. It's different for different people. For Billy it's obviously talking, relating his morning coffee at the diner downtown. "I enjoy it, just a bunch of us old guys telling jokes, mulling over our missions."

"Were you in the Air Force?" I ask, not turning my head. I am now cycling uphill on a country road. I hear my raspy breath from the cigarettes I'd recently tossed in the trash.

"No, infantry, World War Two," he says, loosening his suspenders, taut over a belly the size of a ripe watermelon.

"Oh," I say to be polite. Not saying anything more. But Billy says more. He can't help saying more. I guess it's his nature to say more. That's his happiness.

"Just think," he says, his eyes misting over, "today I'm here. Not too long ago I was on the bathroom floor. Burst appendix just knocked me over. Now you'd think someone my age, someone ninety years old, wouldn't have a burst appendix. That's for young people."

"Who found you?"

"No one. I managed to crawl along the tile somehow. Get myself to a phone. Dial 911. And that wasn't easy either. My hands were shaking so bad, my body one big belt of pain."

Now there's one thing I didn't want to hear was more pain. Everyone in this gym beyond a certain age has a history of it. And they're only too anxious to tell you about it, review every tiny spasm. Show any sign of empathy and you're in for an hour's worth of aches and pains.

I'm at the top of the hill now starting down, so I'm finally catching my breath. My heart has stopped galloping like an angry horse. (I should've tossed those cigarettes long ago.)

"Oh yes, this place keeps me alive," he smiles. "If I didn't come here every day, work my muscles, what's left of them, I'd die, that's for sure. All these nice people. They keep me going, keep my spirits up."

"That's great." I focus on my screen, cycling now along the river path, congratulating myself for climbing that hill, not stopping for a cigarette break since there's no smoking in the gym.

"Well," he says, straightening up, stale sweat staining his white T–shirt. "I've just enough time to visit my wife before the sun sets."

"Where is she?" I say taking a slug from my water bottle, relishing the moisture on my tongue, parched from years of smoking.

"In that pretty park across the way. Been there a long time now. Juvenile diabetic. Doc chopped her legs off at the knees. But that didn't stop her. I bought her some prosthetics. She strutted around on them like Miss Universe. Yeah, she was a tough gal all right. I love to watch the sunset dapple her headstone all pink and yellow. Makes my day."

I suddenly couldn't see the screen. I stopped cycling.

Lonnie the Vet

JW Goll

"We are living in the utopia we deserve," said Lonnie the vet. "It's a vulgar utopia, nothing but beauty mixed with shit and contempt. Idealism ground up in a nonsense machine." I ate my sandwich in silence, like the rest of the crew. We gave the floor to Lonnie whenever he wanted it, partially in deference to his service in Vietnam, but also in awe of his florid melancholy and his tendency to work himself into a rage over nothing whatsoever. "At least we're not living in hell though," he continued. "I know what hell is and hell's not this boring, but it smells a lot worse." The rest of us nodded our heads and kept eating.

Most days my girlfriend brought my lunch to the cemetery where I worked on the ground crew. Now it seems excessive, but it just shows the place we were at in our relationship. We'd make out for a few minutes before she complained that I smelled like gasoline or grass clippings and took off. That should give you an idea of where we were headed. Springdale was a three thousand acre cemetery built along a wooded bluff that overlooked the industrial part of town and the river beyond. The worst part of the job was the poison ivy. The best part was watching the thunderstorms roll in from across the river. When it rained we took cover in an abandoned mausoleum which had a large picture of Jesus still hanging in the entryway. There was mildew growing behind the glass, turning the son of god gray and crinkly, suggesting that our savior lived to be 93 and not 33, skipping the crucifixion altogether. The crypt was cluttered with empty bottles of Richard's Wild Irish Rose and Mogen David Blackberry wine. Once Lonnie found a gold mezuzah buried amongst the empties and handed it to me. "Keep it," he said. "Talismans are bad luck. They never mean what you think they do."

Lonnie bragged a lot about his success with women which was difficult to swallow due to his mopey look and obvious self-disgust. He had a standing offer to go to the Lady Slipper to watch him pick up girls, but nobody took him up on it. Instead we bought six packs and drank them sitting on crypts while the sun went down. It wasn't much of a job but most of us were in no hurry to leave the place after work. One time around dusk we caught a couple of teenagers who climbed up the bluff to knock over gravestones. We corralled them and let Lonnie tell a few of his Nam stories about tiger cages and sliced off lips until one of the kids started to cry. Then, to cheer them up, he told them about the Vietnamese basket fuck, which didn't help matters much. Before we cut them loose Lonnie offered to take them to the Lady Slipper to look at girls, but they declined the offer and slid down the bluff much faster than they'd hiked up.

After a three-week drought, the grass stopped growing and I was laid off. I found another job in a tire shop that cheated customers by selling retreads as new tires. It paid better and I was out of the heat and weather, but the boss was abusive and liked to tell racist jokes to the white customers, most of whom seemed to enjoy them. My girlfriend brought me lunch once or twice but the place creeped her out so she quit coming. We broke up soon after so it didn't make much difference. When the boss learned that she'd left me he said, "Quit whining, better off without that kike." I said I didn't think she was Jewish. "Kid, I can smell Jew pussy with a bucket over my head. You dodged a bullet, count your blessings."

In late summer I returned to Springdale after work with some Pabst and a half empty pint of Jack Daniels. It didn't rain at all in August and even the truncated crew didn't have much to do other than scrape graffiti off the gravestones. Lonnie was in good form. He said he didn't care whether Nixon or McGovern won the coming election because voting was just the suggestion box of slaves. "It's like stomach cancer pretending to be a cure for lung cancer," he said, "anarchy is the only glimmer of hope we have." One of the crew said that anarchy didn't sound so sweet to him. "Yea, well it could benefit from some marketing, for sure."

The crew drifted away and by the time it was dark only Lonnie and I remained. Lonnie lost momentum and became more melancholy. He seemed genuinely saddened to hear that I broke up with my girlfriend. "Filling a girl-shaped hole can be the work of a lifetime," he said. I told him I didn't think it was that kind of relationship. For once he didn't have anything to say and my response seemed to increase his sadness. He told me he never liked the night because he was a poor sleeper. "I never could get the late hours to work for me," he said, "I just got no balance in the dark."

So we sat for a while and didn't talk. I recall him saying, "I wish I didn't see the things I saw or do the things I did," but that might just be my imagination looking for a story, like forming constellations out of random stars. After that: the quiet crackle of prematurely brown leaves falling from oaks; the second shift lunch whistle from the Westinghouse plant; heat lightning that looked like varicose veins; the slow moving yellow lights of a barge plowing upstream; warm, damp air rising from below the bluff; the sound of Lonnie sobbing. When we walked away we left two cans of Pabst on a stone for the tramps who lived in the woods. For good luck.

Regrets of a Washoholic

Matt Potter

Written on the top left–hand corner, inside front cover of the 240–page exercise book: 21st June 1987.

The sticky tape holding the first label in place (on page 1) is a little yellow with age, not yet brown after thirty–three years.

The print on that first label (on page 1) is a clear and gentle reminder.

Care Instructions.
Cold water wash only.
Do not dry clean.
Warm iron.
Made in Australia.

Under that, in blue ink, in my own twenty–one–year–old writing, is the date: 23.6.87.

And the label is stuck smack dab in the centre of the page, exactly in place, measured to the millimetre.

(I was single at the time.)

(And determined that, rather than suffer irritating scratchy tags, I would cut or snip or pick them all off.)

(A helpful note: The key to long–lasting clothing? Follow the washing instructions.)

And under the date I wrote: 'black polo shirt'.

I smile. No size. No place of purchase. I would have travelled on the bus. I would have pulled the polo shirt from its coathanger, slipped it over my head in the changing room. I would have smoothed it over my chest, settled it over my hips and looked at the thin thing looking back at me in the mirror.

Everyone wore black then and I did too.

Everyone wears black now and I don't.

I also had more hair (on my head) then.

I flip the page over. A ringed 2 – so ② – appears in the bottom left–hand corner, and a ringed 3 – so ③ – graces the bottom right–hand.

I gaze at the double spread. I know – I *know* – that each page is numbered thus, continuing to page 240 at the very end.

Smack dab in the centre of page 2, stuck insistently in place, is another label:

Care Instructions.

Warm water wash only.

Do not dry clean.

Warm iron.

Made in Australia from 100% cotton.

And then on page 3:

Care Instructions.

HAND WASH or DRY CLEAN ONLY.

Made in Australia.

100% rayon.

I don't remember the 28.6.87 'beige polo top' from page 2 – beige? me? – but I do remember the rayon on page 3 – 28.6.87 'olive green jacket' – bought on sale on sale on sale for $50.00.

Nothing on the page tells me the jacket cost $50.00, but I remember.

Plus, I never made the HAND WASH or DRY CLEAN ONLY mistake again.

I flick through the book, stop at random: page 52.

'Purple pink yellow pinstripe long–sleeved shirt'.

The label still has a string of holes along its edges, where I unpicked it from the inside neck of the shirt. Under the date – 12.1.90, still in blue ink – is an 'S', inside a blue ink square.

This means I pulled a number of items from department store racks, stepped into the changing room, and – in a blur of pulling on, pulling off, sweaty palms and sticky armpits – slipped out of the store wearing an extra shirt under the shirt I wore in. Smoothed down inner layers and puffed up outer ones, so you couldn't spy extra thickness or creases.

Shoplifting stopped with the new boyfriend in February 1990. (No labels from that month. Too busy fucking!)

Page 53 starts the doubling of labels. Two to a page, in opposite corners, conserving space, sensing my fashion journey's stretching to a long one.

Fashion ... or style?

I waved goodbye to fashion in 1990, aged 24, and decided style was more my thing.

From page 72 onwards, you will find no rayon. No nylon. No polyester. Only cotton and wool, and leather for shoes. Or mohair. Or alpaca.

And later, from 1996 (see page 88) when business shirts – many striped, some bold prints, some crisp, some soft, all beautiful – became my work thing, polycotton earns a mention.

POLYCOTTON

Hand wash or very gentle machine wash.

Warm water and add fabric softener during final rinse cycle.

Machine dryable at very low temperature,

remove as soon as dry.

But *business* shirts only. Their labels now three and four a page, or a list of dot points under one label because I bought the same design on the same day at the same end of financial year sale, in six colours:

- pale orange thin stripe
- dark green medium stripe
- pale yellow w. red relief stitching on collar
- pink, purple and white stripe
- pale green w. dark green buttons
- bright yellow, white cuffs

(I wish I'd snapped photographs of those beautiful shirts, before I outgrew them and sold them for $2.00 each at a garage sale held at my mother's house because I knew they'd fetch a better return in her neighbourhood.)

I slide my hand under the back of the book and it flips open to page 211.

I'm a bit older.

'17.7.16'

I'm a bit fatter.

'Blue Bonds t—shirts x 6, size L', and written in black ink!

I never wore blue but that's all I've worn for years now. Jeans, jackets. Lots of t—shirts. (No long—sleeved shirts hang in my wardrobe.) Page after page after page of blue.

I flick to page 225.

CARE INSTRUCTIONS
WARM MACHINE WASH (MAX 60°C)
DO NOT BLEACH
DO NOT TUMBLE DRY
DO NOT DRY CLEAN
WARM IRON INSIDE OUT
MADE IN CHINA

21.11.18

I open to page 240.

The final page.

Fresh, faded, BLANK.

I've always worn bright socks – even now at age 54 – but now there's only one label needed for 30 socks, 15 pairs, all bought yesterday, all highly–patterned, all noisily cheery, all gloriously loud.

'26.6.20', I write, in black ink, then no dot points, just '15 pairs', then stretch sticky tape around the cardboard label's edges, smoothing it out as I press with the heel of my hand.

CARE INSTRUCTIONS
TURN SOCKS INSIDE OUT BEFORE WASHING
WARM MACHINE WASH (40°C/104°F)
DO NOT BLEACH
DO NOT TUMBLE DRY
MADE IN TURKEY

I flip the completed book shut.

This 240–page book has lasted me 33 years.

How many years will a new book need to last?

Johnny O'Keefe – A Life in One Night

Doug Jacquier

By the time I met the Australian rock legend Johnny O'Keefe in 1977, I was working as a roadie for a middle–of–the–road pub band called Haydown. They played the classic hits that suburban and country audiences wanted to hear. Hardly rock and roll heaven, but it was work. Johnny had been booked to sing at the Marysville pub, with Haydown as his backing band.

As the band travelled to Marysville, everyone was excited to be working with a household name, albeit someone who had long been considered a has–been. Johnny had presented the TV shows *Six O'Clock Rock* and *Sing Sing Sing* in the late '50s and early '60s. He was more of my older sister's era but everyone knew about Johnny and his music, as well as his psychiatric issues, his car crashes and his battles with drugs and alcohol. The tsunami of the Mersey sound and US West Coast rock swept over him in the mid–'60s and his career never recovered.

As the band was setting up, Johnny's manager arrived and, handing out sheet music and a running list, said there would be no rehearsals or sound check. I remember him using the phrase 'it's not rocket science'. Which was just as well, because the lead guitarist was the only one who could read music and he would signal and mouth the chord and key changes as needed during the show.

The place was packed, including a large contingent of men with slicked–down ducktail haircuts and women with wide skirts supported by half a dozen starched white petticoats. In country towns history lives.

The band had worked their way through their usual sets and now it was time for Johnny. The only spotlight the pub had was trained on him as he made his entrance, resplendent in his tailored red suit. Our lead guitarist intoned 'Ladies and gentlemen, the king of Australian rock and roll, Mr. Johnny O'Keefe' and the crowd rose as one as he launched into a strangely stiff and unwild version of 'The Wild One'.

As he progressed through all the old hits like 'She's My Baby', 'I'm Counting on You', 'Move Baby Move' and 'She Wears My Ring', I could sense an unease in the crowd. Like me, they seemed to be thinking 'well, he's here but he isn't', but they were tempering their disappointment out of respect for The King and what the tickets had cost them.

There was the usual fake finish and the crowd played their part in demanding more. He was going to finish with his famous call–and–response hit, 'Shout', allowing the audience to vocalise their devotion.

And that was when disaster struck for me and for Johnny. He was halfway through the famous opening sustained holler of 'We–e–e–e–e–e–ll' when his microphone died.

With no time to find the fault, I ran to the stage, grabbed the protesting lead guitarist's mike and trailed the lead out to Johnny, who was standing motionless and impassive in the middle of the floor, staring a thousand yards into the distance. As I handed the mike to him, scarlet from head to toe, I said lamely, 'Sorry, Johnny'. As I looked into his vacant and unresponsive eyes he mumbled, 'That's alright, mate'.

I scrambled back to my desk, praying to the God of Roadies that everything would work out. And it did. 'W–e–e–e–e–e–ll, you know you make me wannna shout …..'

After the standing ovation and the refusal of more encores, Johnny's manager bundled him into a car and they sped off into the night. Within a year, in 1978, Johnny was dead from a drug overdose, at the age of 43. And the Marysville pub burnt down in the Black Saturday fires of 2009.

My Night in the Big House

Phillis Ideal

Outside my cell, I heard a loud commotion: jangling keys, clinking chains, doors buzzing, overlapping voices, and the guard's keys, hitting the metal doors. Abruptly, the sound of footsteps stopped, the key turned in the lock, and the metal door swung open. I was cuffed and shackled and marched with twenty other prisoners to the sentencing hearing. I was the only light–skinned person and wondered, "*Don't white people commit crimes?*" The line of prisoners looked like shadows: a tattooed tribe covered with crosses, swastikas, serpents, knives, and tears. I kept walking, my palms sweating. It all seemed like a pit stop into a nightmare.

All of the men, the guards, and the prisoners, knew one another. I overheard a guard talking to a prisoner as he cuffed and chained him.

"How is your sister? Is she still single? I always thought she was hot."

"Aw, her old man got busted for drugs. She has a couple of kids and is getting a divorce. She is living with my mother."

The only other woman prisoner, a tall Native American, and I slowed our pace to walk down the hall together and entered the sentencing room. We exchanged sidelong glances and slid next to one another on the back row, looking at the array of men sitting in folding chairs in front of us. I faced her and broke the silence, "Why are you here?"

"I could not pay my fines, so there was a warrant out for my arrest. I will work my time off in jail."

"How long will you be here?"

"I have done this many times, and this time I will be here for two weeks. I have seen most of the inmates in the room. They will stay in jail because they can't pay their fines or afford bail."

"Is there anything for you to read in jail?" After these words came out of my mouth, I felt foolish and naïve, as if I thought jail was a waiting room in a doctor's office stocked with up-to-date magazines. I liked her and hoped she could avoid bouncing off all the various hostilities.

"There are some torn up magazines that I have seen before. Why are you here?"

"I was arrested on a DWI. I am a senior and never been in jail before."

"New Mexico is rough on DWI's. Do you have an attorney?"

"Yes."

When the female guard was handcuffing me for the walk back to the cell, I told her that the judge said I could be released late in the day, so asked her, "Do you know what time I will be released today?"

"I know my job," she said proudly with a sneer, "and it is not to answer your stupid questions, Missy. We may not release you today at all, so don't count on it. Don't count on it, period."

For hours, I sat on my bed, wrapped in my thin blanket, tormented by solitude and the cold. Though I was bone-tired, I compulsively reviewed each detail of the previous night:

242

dinner with friends, the mistake of accepting that second drink, the sirens and flashing lights, failing the sobriety test, and the arrest, followed by the five–hour booking process. Then solitary confinement, wearing a prison–issued green jumpsuit and gripping my ID number. I remembered the induction officer at the prison asked me if I was suicidal. Searching for irony to soften this harsh reality and get a smile, I answered, "Not until now."

The potential humor quickly dissolved, and he retorted, "Don't say that or I will have to put you in that," and pointed to a white straitjacket, hanging from a nail on the wall. As he cycled through his questionnaire and found this was my first arrest, and that I was a 73–year–old retired professor, his tone softened. "I am going to put you in the mental health section. You will have a single cell. You will be safer there."

Screams and a gruesome choir of pain pierced the suffocating silence. The room blurred; edges dissolved into soft and mushy shapes, and the harsh glare of the neon light cast a green glow on the grey walls and the floor. I closed my eyes tightly and opened them a moment later to gain definition. I focused on a haunting silhouette of someone's shadow, traced on the wall. As my eyes searched the four walls, I saw "*Candy loves Cowboy*" scribbled in dark letters on the wall above my bed, and then noticed *"Trixie gives deadhead"* scratched in shaky cursive script on the metal door. There was a tiny scrawled sentence above the toilet, but no matter how much I squinted, I could not make it out, so I slid off the bed and walked over to the toilet to get a better look.

Then, I saw, "*Jesus Saves.*"

Henry, Annie, and Me

Karen Walker

Notices in The Hastings Herald 1880—1940
REF 919.4813 Ale LH
Hastings County History Reading Room

Page 276
Henry Allen, son of Mr. and Mrs. William Allen of Belleville, passed away Saturday, November 16th, 1918, in his twelfth year, of the Spanish Flu now widely seen. Taken sick only four days, the physician could not avert the sad end.

"Here it is, Lizzie," Will says.

He lays Henry's yellow notebook on the bed.

With school closed—so many students have been afflicted—Henry sat at a little table every morning before chores. I gave him words from the newspaper to practice his spelling. *Remembrance, Infantry, Amiens* about the war, *Malady* and *Quarantine* on the home front.

I open his book.

The handwriting is big and loose. Like how he would stride up the road with arms and legs swinging. The script is mindful, keeping to the ruled lines on the paper. He was a dutiful child.

I find the last letter from his teacher, Mr. Wilson, between the pages.

Henry read the letter aloud to me. He thrilled at the cheerful tales of soldiering in Europe, and I smiled at the admonishments to him from so far away to be a good boy and keep up his studies. We gave thanks that the man was safe and well.

There are sketches in the book. One in red pencil may be the great bonfire on Armistice Day. Will took Henry to town to watch a Kaiser made of straw be set ablaze in the park. He wanted him to remember 11th November all his life.

Henry paraded about the kitchen with a broomstick that night, leading the town band like the resplendent drum major he had seen. Annie danced along behind, baby Peter sat on my knee and clapped. How we cheered the end of the war!

"Mr. Wilson will come home now, Momma," Henry said.

He was marking the days inside the back cover.

I close Henry's book, hold it in my arms as I did him. In a corner of our dark bedroom, Will cries.

Page 278

November 22nd. Flu again entered the home of Mr. and Mrs. William Allen and took an angel but five years old, only daughter Anna. Given the current circumstances, no public funeral can be held.

Annie saw a mask in town. It was during one of the Saturday trips she so enjoyed with her father.

Following the public safety notice posted in his window, Mr. Shane was serving customers at the drygoods store with a white cotton cover across his face.

Annie didn't seem to know him. When he exclaimed, as he always did, "Good day, Miss Allen," and offered a peppermint, she stared with big blue glass eyes and then hid her face in Will's coat.

On the journey home, she asked why the man was wearing the mask.

Will explained it would keep him safe from the Flu. What happened to Henry would not befall him.

She nodded. She was a sensible child.

One afternoon, Annie decided that her china doll should wear a mask to a toy tea party.

I cut a square from a linen handkerchief, pinned bits of blue ribbon to the corners. Annie giggled at the smile I drew on the mask. Our girl dotted on freckles just like her own.

Drifting in and out of her mind—she suffered from delirium; Henry had laid so still—Annie could not be comforted. She pushed me away when I kissed her, swatted as I laid cool cloths on her fevered brow and wiped the bloody mucus she coughed. Will brought the doll, still in its little mask.

"Take it off, Poppa," she cried. "I can't see her pretty face."

I hear them on the porch beneath the bedroom window: little Peter, Will, and my sister Nell come so quickly after our desperate call.

"Where is Momma?" Peter asks.

Someday he will be tall, like his father.

Will chokes, then steadies his voice. "Look, here is Auntie."

"I want Momma!"

"Be brave," my husband says.

They both are.

"What an adventure you will have, son, riding in a motor car! Not like our old buggy, is it?"

My sister is sobbing. "I want to see Lizzie."

No, Nell. My nightclothes, the beautiful quilt you made as our wedding gift are soaked and stained. My skin is grey and cold, but I am burning. There is an awful war raging in my chest: it is defeating me. But the worst pain—what I cannot endure—is that Henry and Annie felt this.

"The doctor says no one should go in," Will tells her. "Take Peter away."

Thank you, sister.

There are quick footfalls on the stairs, then a rush of air as Will opens the door.

I must know.

He leans close as I can only whisper now.

"Did you send Peter with his teddy bear? Did you tell Nell that if he awakens in the night, she should rub his back and hum a soft song? Peter's feet are always chilly. Be sure he wears two pairs of warm socks."

Will sweeps my hair—a clinging, maddening spider's web—from my face. "Can the doctor come back?"

He strokes my hand and says, "I don't know. There are so many—"

"The minister?"

He kisses my cheek. I can ask for no more.

Page 282

Never in the history of our Town did the records of mortality fill so rapidly as of the Spanish Flu these days just past. Among the lost on Monday last, December 2nd, Elizabeth Isabel, dear wife of Mr. William Allen and mother of two lamented children. All thus removed from our midst, consigned to the earth in mere weeks. We grieve.

My Little Sales Boy

Marwan F. Al-Sheriffi
translated by Essam M. Al-Jassim

Just like she does every morning, Fatimah bids a fond farewell to her ten-year-old son after helping him lift a large bag of homemade delights onto his small back—the treats destined to be sold at the village market. Quietly stepping onto the woven mat, she prays Allah will bless her son with a bountiful livelihood, as well as bodily strength, particularly for his back, which has become bowed from regularly carrying such heavy loads.

With quick, energetic steps, the agile boy nimbly skips and twists his way through the narrow paths and alleys to reach the village center. He then takes his usual place and loudly hawks his *samboosah* and *saltah*. Pleasant aromas of the foodstuffs' fragrant flavors waft from his bag, while absolute joy and contentment illuminate his face. Suddenly, a wave of light and sound washes away his voice. For a moment, the explosion of a suicide bomber paralyzes the area, then utter pandemonium sweeps through the marketplace.

When the military police arrive, they find the woman, who had prayed to Allah just that morning to bless her son, weeping bitterly over a bloodied, headless, mangled little corpse, cradling young shoulders that cheerfully used to bear such tremendous weight.

Sam Schuman's "Swim of My Life"

Samuel Schuman and Sandy Schuman

"When did I first start working? I guess it was in Atlantic City at the age of ten. My father had no work in Philadelphia at all, and so he went to Atlantic City, 60 miles away. It's now a casino gambling area, but then, in the '10s and '20s, it was in its heyday. It was the choice vacation spot of the rich and famous. Did they vacation in Florida? It was swamps and alligators back then, and no air conditioning. Hawaii? It wouldn't become a state for another 45 years; getting there by boat took probably 10 days! Atlantic City? It was just a train ride from the major metropolitan areas of the United States, and that was when trains were at their finest. Atlantic City was beautiful, dignified, quiet, and lovely. They called it 'The World's Playground'.

"My father's job was pushing these comfortable, rolling benches, with wicker seats and backs. They could seat two or three people, and he'd push them along the Atlantic City Boardwalk for miles and miles. Most of the fee the tourists paid went to the company; sometimes the tips compensated for the poor pay.

"After my father had been doing this for a couple of weeks, he sent for my older brother and me, because he saw other boys selling newspapers on the Boardwalk and making good money."

Today, of course, people check the news on their phones. Back then, only one person in fifteen had a telephone, and it weighed several pounds and hung on the wall. A three–minute call from New York to Boston cost two dollars, almost fifty dollars today. (You couldn't call New York to San Francisco; that line wasn't built yet.) Television news? It was three decades away. You couldn't even get news on the radio; that didn't happen until the 1920s. So, vacationers bought the local newspapers: *The Philadelphia Inquirer, The Philadelphia Press, The Philadelphia Record, The Philadelphia Bulletin.*

"My brother and I joined the other boys traversing the Boardwalk selling newspapers. They normally sold for two cents but out there on the Boardwalk we got a nickel, and we waxed rich, sometimes making as much as thirty or forty cents a day! We had quite an experience there. We worked all day long— selling the morning, afternoon, and evening editions—every day. Except Sunday. We didn't sell the Sunday papers because they were heavy, expensive, and hard to get. And because Atlantic City was 'The World's Playground', visitors came from all over. While they would settle for the local paper during the week, on Sundays they wanted their hometown paper. They'd go to a store on the Boardwalk where they'd have racks and racks of newspapers from all over the country, all over the world. On Sundays, my brother and I were out of business.

"Thank God, we were out of business! Here we were, two city boys, working on the beach all summer long. If we didn't have a chance to go swimming at least one day in the week, it would have been torture.

"One particular Sunday, we were very eager to go swimming. The weather was very bad—cloudy, dark, sprinkles of rain—but we didn't want to miss out on our swim, so we went out to where my father was working, at Pacific Avenue and the Boardwalk, in front of a big hotel, long since gone, the Royal Palace. It was a large, four-story hotel made completely of wood, right on the beach. In front of the hotel, a good distance out in the ocean, was a raft.

"This particular Sunday, when we went out to swim, there was not a soul in the water, not a soul on the beach. You'd have to be crazy to go swimming on that day, the weather was so bad. But this was our precious one day of the week to swim. So, we went into the locker room, put on our swimsuits, and walked onto the beach and into the water. My brother said, 'Come on Sam, let's swim out to the raft.' So, we swam out to the raft, which was not so difficult for him, five years older, but more than a bit of a swim for me.

"The minute we got on the raft, hell broke loose. Bolts of lightning streaked across the sky like you've never seen before and you're lucky if you didn't. You see such lightning today only in movies, in documentaries, or in textbooks. The more time that passed the more scared I became, and finally my brother said, 'Let's go.' He didn't look around at me, he just belly-flopped into the water and made for the beach, which was only just about visible; the raft seemed to have traveled a few miles out to sea. I stayed on the raft, too scared to jump in.

The farther away my brother swam, the more scared I got. The wind blew harder, the waves grew bigger and choppier, the streaks of lightning and cracks of thunder more terrible. I watched as he swam further and further away. I lost sight of him. I couldn't see him. I couldn't see the beach. I couldn't stand the terror. Finally, I jumped in and began to swim. I swam for all I was worth, though not sure of the right direction. After a while I felt neither my arms nor legs. It must have been instinct that drove me to continue going toward that beach.

"I don't know how many minutes or hours it was. All I know is that I landed somewhere enough out of the water to breathe, and laid there, limp. After a while, I had no idea of the time, I heard my brother say, 'Let's go, Sam,' and he took off to the locker room to get dressed. I dragged myself after him. I recall to this day, sixty—eight years later that it was the swim of my life, which I shall never forget."

River and the Cathedral

Leah Rogin

"I never wanted to come here."

"It matters to me, so it should matter to you."

"Sitting in the square drinking coffee matters to me, but we never seem to do it."

"Come on, River, don't be so lazy. We didn't come half–way around the world just to sit around and drink coffee."

"Maybe you didn't."

"Just look at the light. And the glass, the way it makes the light change color when it filters through it. It's amazing."

"I don't like it."

"You don't like anything."

"I don't like churches."

"It's not a church, it's a cathedral."

"All I see are zombie–Jesuses everywhere."

"Keep your voice down, River, this is a holy place."

"I don't give a fuck."

"If you're going to be like this, let's just leave."

"I'd like to, I'd really like to."

"Well, go then. I'll meet you back at the hotel later."

"I'll be in the square, drinking coffee."

"I knew this was a mistake."

"Dragging me to Italian Renaissance painting after painting, when all I wanted to do in Italy was eat pasta and drink espresso? Or following that up with church after cathedral when you know how I feel about religion?"

"No, coming to Europe with you. You just don't get it. It's not about religion, it's about history."

"Oh, I'm so sorry that I didn't study art history, that I don't see anything but boring pictures of fucking stupid Mary who was just delighted to be pregnant and never had a second of goddamn morning sickness."

"Do you feel sick?"

"Not right now, but I'm just saying."

"You wanted to come to Europe, remember?"

"Yeah, but just because I wanted to at least see a different country before I'm chained to a kitchen table for the next 18 years doesn't mean that I want to hang out in fucking churches all day."

"Just leave. People are staring."

"Okay, I'll see you around somewhere."

"Don't be like that."

"May I please have my passport?"

"For what?"

"Just in case, I might need it."

"Are you leaving?"

"If you're staying, I'm leaving. Now give me my fucking passport."

"Great, now the guard is coming over to talk to us. Thanks for making a scene, River."

"You're the one making the scene. Give me my passport!"

"Let's just go. I just thought you'd appreciate the stained glass, the way the light comes through. I just wanted to show you something that's special to me."

"I never asked for a fucking cathedral."

"That's true, you never did."

Margaret Reed

Rita Wilson

Aunt Marg never wore pants a day in her life. On frigid winter days when she was needed at the dairy barn, she plodded her way through the snow in worn leather boots, layers of skirts, and her wool coat swishing around her calves. Even as my husband, John, and I went to visit his great aunt in her waning years, when her contemporaries wore elastic–waisted tan polyester pants from Blair House, Aunt Marg preferred a wool cardigan, a long denim skirt, and brown oxfords.

Aunt Marg and Uncle Curt lived on an eight–acre plot in Chippewa, Pennsylvania, upon which they built their ranch house, a milk house, a small apartment building, and a sheep barn. After Uncle Curt's death, John and I visited more frequently. I loved to roam the yard, with its brambles and herbs, pungent weeds, dried pods, and ripe berries, and I was especially captivated by the milk house where, in its heyday, white milk, chocolate milk, cottage cheese and buttermilk were produced. Now the sun forced its way through the cloudy windows of the barn–like structure, illuminating dust particles floating in the massive spaces above the old oak worktables. Drafty and dusty, the milk house smelled of dried wood and pungent dried herbs and flowers, housing Aunt Marg's collections of pure wool, colored glass, rocks in old glass milk jars, dyed burlap, and musty manuals and herb encyclopedias.

256

She proudly showed us the poster she created for the Herb Society – a large board, greyed at the edges, but decorated in the middle with petite round colored coils of yarn, spun by Aunt Marg from wool from her Suffolk sheep that she herself sheared. She had dyed these yarn samples rich emerald, vibrant crimson, deep purple, and pale lavender, with herbs that she grew.

After the milk house tour, Aunt Marg led us up the back steps to the kitchen, where the aroma of fresh–baked apple bread hung in the air. John and I crowded around the ancient woodblock table in her cramped kitchen. From the kitchen window, we could watch the wooly white Suffolk sheep with their handsome black faces roam the fields behind the milk house. Aunt Marg opened the oven door and took out the apple bread she made from the fruits on her trees. The teakettle whistled, and we drank herbal tea while waiting for the apple bread to cool, and Aunt Marg began one of her captivating tales.

My favorite story involved Aunt Marg in search of a rare herb she wanted to transplant to her garden, which she claimed only grew on mountainsides. One story version has her joyfully discover the mysterious herb growing on the side of a cliff; Curt hangs onto her legs as she dangles dangerously over the cliffside to retrieve the precious herb. In another version, she is in the grip of a mysterious companion, suspended over the cliffside, while he lies on the cliff, lowering her down inch by inch over the weeds, rocks, and hills below, as she reaches down to retrieve the precious herb. She ends this story with a chuckle and a twinkle in her eyes. Aunt Marg knew every herb that grew in Western Pennsylvania. She categorized them, spoke to garden clubs about them, cooked with them, brewed tea with them, and used them medicinally. No over-the-counter medicines cluttered her bathroom cabinet – not even when she broke her hip at the age of 85. Her doctor told her that the healing process would take several months. Not one to be sidelined for a week, let alone months, Aung Marg took matters into her own hands, rehabbing herself on a sturdy old foot-pedal loom. When I stepped on the loom, I couldn't even budge the pedal.

When Aunt Marg was in her nineties, she sold her last four sheep, no longer able to care for them herself. The five-foot tall sheep barn made of weathered grey barn siding had at one point housed eight or nine sheep. John went to visit her one morning, stopping at Dunkin' Donuts to pick up some blueberry muffins. Her baking days and her wool-dyeing days may have been over, but she could still spin a yarn. She put the coffee on for John while heating water for her tea. John sat at the familiar kitchen table and glanced out the window beyond the back yard to an empty space where the sheep barn had been.

"Aunt Marg," John said, "what happened to the sheep barn?"

Aunt Marg's face crinkled into a smile. "I buried it."

"You did what?

"Well, I buried it!"

"You buried it?"

She nodded with a mischievous grin.

"How? Why?"

"Well, I wanted to burn it, but the township wanted $100 for a permit. So, I called Phil, and he brought over his backhoe.

We dug a hole, and he knocked the barn down, and we pushed it into the hole and buried it!"

Great Aunt Margaret died at the age of 98, when her heart and mind ultimately surrendered. John and I had the chance to buy her property, with its charming milk house, and acres of wildflowers, herbs, trees, and wildlife. We sadly realized that it was too far from the city and would require a tremendous change of lifestyle – one which we were not prepared to make. In retrospect, I believe we made the right decision. I admire Aunt Marg's strength, spirit, capability, and resilience, but I am not clever in the ways in which she was.

The property was sold to a development company who cleared the land to build five houses. When they dug into the area behind the main house, they found, buried in the dirt, rough–hewn pieces of grey barn wood.

Terry

Liam J. Blackley

She's the kind of person you could tell any story about, no matter how outrageous, and people would believe it.

Her sisters pull back in surprise as she plants a pump on her chair, stepping up onto the table, surprising the band and the restaurant's other guests alike. They're somewhere in Quebec, dining cordially with their bottles of red wine.

Bending to the centrepiece, she tugs out a red rose and gently pinches it between her teeth. One foot stomps down, her hands fanning out around her, the dress spinning like a showgirl's. It's a flamenco, everyone in the room realizes. The band is missing notes from laughing. Both sisters grip the table to steady it for her, grinning but a bit flushed themselves, some combination of wine and attention. Her hand raises, waving hello to God as her heels dig into the wood of the table.

One evening with long shadows, she'll explain to her great-nephew that she loved only once, from a distance. And she loved him enough that when he didn't choose her, she waved goodbye with a smile and learned to dance by herself.

As a wine glass tumbles off the table for a sister to catch, her footing never falters. The stem of the rose never sees so much as a bite mark. Every movement deliberate and complete, until the outside world bumps up against her. Flying feet that never make a mess, nothing left to kick now they've danced the table clean.

In the back of her mind she thinks the band wasn't playing a flamenco, it was probably something French after all, and she lets out a tinkling laugh no one can hear over the music.

This is how everyone in the room will remember her, the story they will tell first when they introduce her, their answer when asked how their Quebecois holiday went. There is a woman–shaped silhouette in the fabric of the world and as she bunches her dress in her fist and her feet leave the table, for a golden second she fills it perfectly.

Sister Baptiste

Lisa Costa

It was autumn in the year of our Lord 1963. Dressed in my plaid Catholic school uniform, I skipped along the five and one−half blocks to school that morning, careful not to step on the sidewalk cracks so as not to "break my mother's back."

I entered the dusty, chalky atmosphere of the school. I sat at the front of the classroom at a stiff, wooden desk and placed my folded hands on the desktop until Sister spoke. Some of the other kids shouted at each other as they entered the room and piled their belongings on the coat rack in the back of the classroom. But I sat in silence until Sister told us to sit down and started the Morning Prayer.

"Amen," the class recited.

Sister Baptiste, a young nun with flawless skin set against the harshness of the veil she wore, began the religion lesson.

"Class, who can recite the first commandment?" Sister asked.

I was first to raise my hand. Not just eager to please her, I wanted to follow in her footsteps when I grew older.

I am the Lord your God. You shall have no other gods before Me, I recited.

As a child, I watched Charlton Heston portray Moses in *The Ten Commandments*. When God talked to Moses, He seemed to come down from the mountain into our living room, Hollywood instilling more fear of the Lord in me than the nuns in school.

As I walked home from school each day, I looked across the street at the other children walking home from a different school. I remembered Sister Agnes telling us, "Those children are the publics. They won't go to heaven when they die, because they don't go to Catholic school and receive the sacraments."

And then, "You shouldn't walk on the same side of the street with them."

I asked Sister Baptiste about what Sister Agnes told us.

"It is not our place to say who will enter the Kingdom of God. We do not judge others. We must pray for them."

The publics didn't look any different than my friends at Catholic School, and I always listened to what Sister Baptiste said.

Second grade was the year of receiving sacraments in the Catholic religion. Roman Catholics believe that bread and water are transformed into the body and blood of Christ during the ritual of the Mass, and followers of the Church receive the body of Christ in the form of a wafer, called the Eucharist. The taste of the wafer was the topic of discussion among my classmates, but I was more concerned with my dress for the occasion.

On the morning of my First Communion, my class had to report to the church classroom at 6:30 a.m. I couldn't eat breakfast; my stomach hurt.

After Sister Baptiste placed us in the processional line, boys on one side, girls on the other, we started walking down the church aisle to the altar. I reached my assigned seat in the pew.

Then I vomited – down the pristine white lace dress I wore and onto the wooden pews where the other children sat.

As I looked towards my mother, Sister grabbed my hand and escorted me out of the church and into the restroom.

I don't know why I vomited. Maybe I had forgotten one of my sins during confession and thought I would go to hell. But faith in God—or fear of Him—sent me back to the pew to take my place in line to receive the Sacrament of the Holy Eucharist. Vomit scent and all, I knelt at the altar and looked up at the priest, innocent and awed.

My heart broke when Sister Baptiste was transferred to another parish. I visited her new convent and took her teachings with me when my family relocated from Philadelphia to Pittsburgh.

Summer days in 1970 were filled with lazy hours. The importance of appearance consumed my thoughts while I watched Susan Dey sing and play the drums on *The Partridge Family* television show. I was thirteen and dreamed that I could look like her, while trying to absolve myself from the sin of vanity.

Susan's long straight hair hung down her back, free of split ends and frizz. She had clear, alabaster skin like Sister Baptiste. I continually scrubbed my face clean in an effort to emulate their flawless complexions, but for different reasons that created turmoil. Sister's flawlessness led me to believe she was closer to God. Susan Dey attracted the boys and that is what I wanted to do now. I had to look my best. My parents couldn't afford the expensive Catholic high schools in the area we lived, so I would attend the public high school, where the girls wore mini-skirts and hot pants like Susan's. Sister would not be in the classroom making the girls kneel on the floor to ensure that their skirts touched the ground...

It was almost springtime in my seventeenth year when Joey and I drove to the deserted church parking lot. He turned off the engine and climbed in the back seat.

I slid down in the back seat, remembering Sister taught me that God was everywhere and could see what I was doing. I didn't want to go against Sister and her teachings. But Sister wasn't here, even though I thought I saw the outline of her veil in the dark. For now, I was with Joey. I loved him. I trusted him. He smiled, and I knew he thought I was pretty.

He spoke with utter sincerity and conviction, not sounding the least bit nervous. And so, I believed him. Well, why wouldn't I believe him? He was my boyfriend and I was his girlfriend. Boyfriends and girlfriends didn't lie to one another. *Thou shalt not lie* was one of the commandments and Joey was a Catholic.

Years, decades, have passed since that night in Joey's car. I don't go to Mass on Sunday anymore. I divorced my husband. According to the Roman Catholic Church, I have many sins to repent.

But I have never forgotten Sister's teachings, and I know she is in heaven, not judging me, but praying for me.

Luke Kettle's Post–Industrial Wasteland Fairytale

Jonathan Slusher

There was a bad accident somewhere around Exit 2. Thousands of angry motorists crawled along the last miles of New Jersey through a ninety–five–degree mid–August haze. Half–melted tar tugged at the tires of vehicles funneling into Lane 10, a sound that always reminded me of Velcro shoes. The smell, exhaust, heat, and humidity were miserable and I was in the middle of it all. On average 1,200–1,400 patrons would come through this lane in an eight–hour shift. It was filthy, greasy, and disgusting. Modern toll booths—like those three miles south at the Delaware Memorial Bridge—were air conditioned and clean. But the old Exit 1 toll plaza of the New Jersey Turnpike was built in 1948 and hadn't been renovated since.

The day was another slow mover, but not as bad as the day before, when I'd heard a turnpike rumor that I was still a virgin. I wasn't a full timer, just summer help. School started in three more weeks. I didn't want this to be my life. Still, it was a good job with benefits, and that was getting hard to find.

A Peter Pan tour bus departed too quickly and noxious effluvium hung in the air, the cloud expanded, writhing, tumbling—as if it were alive. Carbon Monoxide, Carbon Dioxide, Ozone, some asshole dumped three hundred and five sticky pennies into my hands for a $3.05 toll. A double shot of Golden Earring was coming up after a short commercial break. They sucked! In the parking lot my piece–of–shit brown Oldsmobile Cutlass Supreme with brown interior sat baking in the heat. I was twenty–one and living at home with my overworked single mom. Dad had been gone twelve years now. It was Friday and I had no plans after work.

"How's it going?" I asked the wrong driver.

"I'm Shitty!"

"Have a nice day," I mumbled.

"Drop dead."

It was mostly sunny or partly cloudy depending on how I looked at it. I was more than three quarters of the way through my last day shift. On the brink of three days off, I kept the endless line of exhaust–spewing buses, trucks, and cars flowing through my lane at a steady clip. My battle–worn CD player was blasting Bryter Layter and I worked to the rhythm, moving smoothly, tuning the scenery out as best I could.

How far was it to Baltimore? D.C.? Philadelphia? Excuse me. But do you have any Grey Poupon?

I quick drawled replies like the Sundance Kid. *Seventy miles, one hundred and ten, get off at Exit 3. Grey Poupon?– but of course.*

This was my second summer at the pike. I was finishing up an Associate's Degree in Biology at the community college in the fall, although rumor was that the Turnpike Authority was hiring full timers again. Full timers made good money, real good money, better than a teacher's salary, with a pension that would allow me to retire in twenty years. Combined with the

Roth IRA my mom had started for me, I could have been all set by the time I turned forty–five. Sure, sometimes it sucked, but what job didn't? It was steady income.

If I got offered a job I was seriously considering taking it.

I switched the light over my lane from green to red and started to close out the lane. A blue Camry, two purring BMW bikes, and a Ford SUV rolled through.

Grace pulled up in a Geo Tracker. There were four of them in the car. She was in the back passenger side and was the hardest one to get a good look at. She came within a split second of becoming just a smiling silhouette of red hair in the back seat of a distant high school friend's little sister's rust bucket mobile.

But I acted completely out of character, spontaneously, and relied for once on pure instinct. If I hadn't made that split second decision when I did, my status as the introverted, ball– busting lightning rod of the turnpike toll plaza might have endured forever. And Nick Drake's last album helped break the ice some too.

No one would believe it if I told them that I could somehow pick out her individual sweet and smoky scent through the half open window of an idling car. But it didn't matter if it was or wasn't plausible.

A slightly recognizable skinny blonde handed me the ticket. I knew her from somewhere. Her ticket was from exit 18W. $4.60, I mindlessly made the change.

"Isn't that Nick Drake?" a voice sang from the backseat, "I've never heard this song before."

I handed back the change and tried to look across into the back seat.

"It's *Northern Sky* from Bryter Layter." I glanced inside. "Have the CD. It's just a mix. I can make another one."

"No. I couldn't," she said.

"Sure you can." My eyes found Grace and locked on her.

She leaned forward between the front seats and stretched her freckled hand toward mine.

"What's it like being a toll collector anyway?"

I shrugged. "It sucks."

"Well, we've got room for five." She patted the empty cracked vinyl space next to her.

Wait. She wasn't joking. Grace dared me with her eyes.

I had three more weeks until school. If I bailed now, I'd be strapped for cash by the end of the semester.

"I'm Luke, Luke Kettle." I couldn't think of anything else to say. And I had to say Luke twice or else people often thought my name was Lou.

The girls laughed. They were spending the weekend at a beach house in Dewey Beach, Delaware.

"You should come along," they said.

An oldtimer stared from Lane 11. His small 'o' mouth became a capital 'O' as I jumped in and squeezed into the back seat. They popped in the CD. *Pink Moon* was the first track.

Grace and I sang it together.

I spent the weekend dressed in my turnpike shirt and a pair of cheap board shorts Grace picked out for me. I scored 100,000 on Ms. Pacman at the laundromat. We made out after midnight on a lifeguard stand.

Our first apartment was a studio. The first car we bought was a 1992 diesel VW wagon. We got married on a Friday to save cash because we had a girl on the way. My best man joked in his speech that my life was a white trash South Jersey post–industrial wasteland fairytale.

Everyone laughed.

The best jokes have some truth to them.

Suzanne Visits Vienna 1938

James Sullivan

Suzanne Esther Johnstone left England with an age—old mix of excitement and dread. She crossed the sea to Ostend and boarded her train alone, travelling through Germany for a stint in Vienna. Suzanne soon discovered Europe in 1938 was not everything she had hoped. Moving to the dining car one day, Suzanne met another passenger, one Mr Von. The waiter urged him to join Suzanne and he initially refused, not wanting to intrude.

"Do sit down and lunch with me, 'Mr Dutchman', you are a Hollander, are you not?" she said.

Mr Von raised his eyebrows, *"Why, how did you guess that?"*

They ate and as the conversation deepened, Suzanne couldn't help but ask his views of the rising tensions. Mr Von revealed he had, up until its annexation by Nazi Germany, been living in Austria, and confirmed Suzanne's own opinions. He ventured that England had made the wrong choice, and had they made a stand then the whole world would have been with them against Germany.

"There is an intense hatred prevalent in Holland against Germany, for the Hollanders love their freedom and they can

see the beginning of the end—For the British Empire, whom everyone looked to as the leading nation, has been forced to admit defeat without even a war to Germany."

They passed Nuremburg as they rode, as immense and intimidating as Suzanne could have imagined. With its huge Roman Pillars and Golden Eagle, ringed by swastikas decorating the main entrance. *"A truly marvellous setting for that maniacal creator."* Suzanne could all but imagine the scene; a dark night with the rally grounds packed—thousands upon thousands of people—illuminated by torches as the leaders mounted the steps to entertain the hungry mob. She shuddered.

As Suzanne and Mr Von neared Vienna, they moved to a compartment and were joined by a cheery-faced Austrian whose name escaped her. He had his own news on the state of it all, with Mr Von serving as translator. The man informed them things were bleak in Austria—the only people who were happy were the *"mob"*. Employment was only up because of extensive road building and reconstruction of public buildings, providing little hope of long-term work. The country was poverty-stricken and full of spies. The Austrian had a saying in his circle if someone dared speak too recklessly.

"Hark, did you hear the train whistling for Dachau?" he said to them.

He continued to tell them he was a Government Official. He only kept his job after the annexation by tracing his and his wife's ancestry back to 1720 to show not a drop of Jewish blood could be found. Even then, his son was forced into the Hitler Youth or he would have lost his government position. As they talked a string of people walked past their compartment, seemingly trying to listen in. Three clear strangers—what were they discussing with this Austrian citizen?

Every train reaches its destination though, and so they parted ways at Vienna. Suzanne hustled through the station, surrounded by uniforms and swastikas, charging through for a taxi to her hotel. She had been told by the Austrian that those who curry favour with the Nazi officials wear a Swastika, and those who don't want to simply find the smallest one possible, but they still wear it. Exhausted by the journey, she made ready for bed but heard voices outside her room. She *"looked out the window and behold about a hundred were girls age 9–10 years with swastika banners, marching in four deep and singing some historical song. Their voices were beautiful and harmonised very well. I must admit I enjoyed it but somehow it sounded all wrong."*

Getting up early the next day to explore, she conversed with a hotel waiter and heard the opposite side of the tale: things were great.

"All the poor people have work, there is no unemployment and we have kicked out all the Jews," he said.

"But what about your former leaders, what will happen to them?" she asked.

A shrug. *"They did not worry about us when the country was going from bad to worse, so why should we worry about them?"*

Suzanne pressed further, questioning about the Jews, *"What of them? What will they do? Where will they go?"*

Another indifferent shrug. *"We don't know or care, that is their affair, we don't want them—let England take them, she has plenty of room."*

Disquieted, Suzanne left to see the city. Again, all she saw were *"youths in uniform with rifles on their shoulders hoarding every conceivable public building, red and white banners and black swastikas plastered on every prominent building, even swastikas in the form of baggage labels stuck on just ordinary windows, made me ill, no one looked happy, made me think of a city in deep deep mourning."*

She wandered through the university square and found the same torches and eagles she had glimpsed at Nuremburg, with even the University buildings defaced, and Suzanne felt a pit deepen in her stomach. She walked to St Stephens Cathedral, wanting to cleanse herself spiritually. From there she headed for the shopping district and stumbled across a lovely store run by a brother and sister, cheerful and smiling. Neither wore a swastika, and they planned to stay that way for as long as they could help it.

Suzanne wasn't sure what to think anymore. She'd lived with military and healthcare workers, been around the continent and talked to those of every nation, but what could be done? England had already chosen to appease Germany with the Munich Agreement. *"What happened—we just signed this agreement; received a fair amount of momentary applause and patting on the back for preventing (temporarily) a world war, and then as always does happen a reaction sets in—complete silence from our leaders, not one direct comment, statement, or criticism of how the agreement was being carried out."*

She could see more to come.

Chip and the Bear

Robert Walton

I'm not a sentimentalist about wild animals. I feel that anthropomorphizing them is beyond silly, beyond arrogant, even beyond dangerous; it's just disrespectful. Still, I've come to realize that both the urge and the ability to communicate between species exist. All living creatures may be subject to Darwinian forces, but, when stars align, we may also share an awareness that we're in the struggle together. Kill or be killed? Sure. However, there's more to existence than that. Sometimes we discover parallel paths, shared non−lethal concerns.

Six or seven years ago friend Chip (a younger rock climbing partner − I have none else nowadays) and I spent a day above Tenaya Lake's mesmerizing, emerald depths. With acres of shining Yosemite granite around us, crisp crystals for our fingers and six hundred feet of exhilarating air below our toes, we exalted in pure movement through pure air.

Hours later, our minds still full of the harmonies we'd found up high, we relaxed next to our post climb, post supper, post good bottle of red wine campfire in Tuolumne Meadows. Contemplating a good climb in such fashion is almost as good as climbing it again. I took another sip of wine.

Then nature called. I stepped some yards into the forest's shadow to pee behind a lodgepole pine. I wasn't drunk, but neither was I strictly sober − mellow, rather. Zipping up, I experienced a familiar and not unfriendly push against my left leg. My big dog Barnaby offers just such a rub when he feels I've been ignoring him too long.

I glanced down into a bear's eyes, not Barnaby's. It was a yearling bear − perhaps a hundred pounds. It may have been the wine, but my threshold for being alarmed was not breached. His gaze seemed to convey some plaintive appeal. We looked at each other for a long moment before I finally I asked, "What do you want, bear?" I knew full well that he would cheerfully accept a serving of T−bone steak, ranch beans, garlic bread, Ghirardelli's chocolate, and the last drop of our cabernet, but thought it best to put the ball in his court.

My tone was not harsh, but Mr. Teen Bruin decided I wasn't about to offer him supper leftovers. He slipped away from my side with a last reproachful glance. Not wishing to alarm him, I stood still and let him go where he wanted to go. That happened to be straight to our picnic table next to our fire where Chip stood with his cup of wine.

Teen Bruin looked up at him for a moment and then repeated the convivial push he'd given me. Chip turned, saw who his affectionate visitor was and leapt straight into the air. Feet barely kissing the ground from his first bound, his second bound was more astonishing even than the first and propelled him straight through the campfire's flames. He disappeared before his cup − the spilled wine describing a red rainbow's arc against the firelight − touched the ground or his scream of terror faded into the pines. I guess he hadn't drunk quite enough yet to embrace inter−species communication.

The disappointed and somewhat bewildered bear wandered through shadows toward a distant campfire, leaving me to contemplate Darwin, humans, bears and my last sip of wine.

Cornflowers Were His Favorite

Beate Sigriddaughter

Cornflowers were his favorites. I didn't know my grandfather well. We lived a twelve–hour train ride apart. I remember him slender, quite handsome, soft–spoken, and very kind.

Cornflowers were one of my mother's favorites too. She had told me many times about walking hand in hand with her father after her own mother had died, through wheat fields and rye fields he owned before the war, learning the names of flowers and birds, and learning to trust the comfort of his familiar presence.

When he died suddenly many years later, she was inconsolable. She had taken it for granted he would always be there. There was no one she could leave me with, my father being out of town on business, so she took me along on her journey of saying goodbye.

I remember her tears, the wrenching sound of her sobs. I remember the soot on the windows in the train, the greasy spots on the heavy brown curtains, the dusty smell of unplanned travel.

Her stepmother, only a few years older than my own mother, greeted us with shaky smiles and one of the few hugs that Germans would take the liberty of exchanging in that era of stoic handshakes.

On the day of the funeral there were wreaths of lilies and white roses and fragrant green fir and spruce. My mother looked haunted, pale, and beautiful in her black dress.

With wreaths and seven siblings and extended families and a shortage of cars, some of us walked to the funeral. It wasn't far.

We walked past fields. It was June. Cornflowers were in bloom. I had recently learned how to braid flowers into a wreath. So I plucked flowers from the edge of the fields as we walked and started braiding them to send along with him. Some of them were hard to pluck and scored the skin of my fingers. Still, it was the one useful thing I could think of doing, being small and typically superfluous in the company of adults.

One of my aunts decided to upbraid me: "What a vain child. Here we are going to her grandfather's funeral, and she is making a wreath for her hair."

"No, it's a wreath for his grave," I explained.

She looked as though she didn't believe me or else preferred to stick with her own interpretation. My beautiful sad mother was too busy grieving to come to my aid, and so I had a first lesson in needing to steel myself against a life of much misinterpretation.

Father Francisco

Flemming George

Father Francisco had turned forty. From his cassock pocket, he took out a bag of marijuana. He had confiscated it earlier in the day from Stefano and his younger brother Michael, two privileged altar boys left to their own devices by uncaring parents. He had caught them trying to switch the incense in the church. Father Francisco knew the kids were up to no good when he heard one of them say, 'I like the pope. The pope smokes dope.'

He dropped the bag into his desk drawer and sat down to enjoy the quiet of his office. He began to unwrap a birthday present left for him by his friends. As he tore away the gold paper, he was touched to find the gift was a box of Kentucky Cheroots. He opened the box and removed one of the cigars. He took a lighter from his cassock pocket and sat back in his chair. He held the cigar in his hand and placed the lighter on the desk.

Father Francisco had served the Catholic Church for twenty years and smoked cigars for twenty–five years. He often joked that smoking was his vocation and religion was his vice. In 1997 when Francisco was eighteen, he'd studied at a film school. The film tutor split the students into several groups for each to complete a short film project. By chance, Father Francisco found himself in the same group as a young man from California, also called Francisco. This Francisco knew much more about the world than Father Francisco. He had written several letters to Bill Clinton calling for the legalization of a number of drugs including marijuana and cocaine. The younger Father Francisco admired his liberal attitudes.

One afternoon, following a talk on violence in the films of Sam Peckinpah, they wondered down to St James's Park. Father Francisco lit a cigar. He offered one to his new friend. He was surprised to see his friend hollow out the cigar and load it with marijuana.

'It's called a blunt,' he said to Father Francisco, 'do you want to try some?'

'No thanks, I will stick with this,' he answered, holding up his own cigar.

Father Francisco watched him take a long pull on the blunt. Francisco held in the smoke for a few seconds and then coughed and laughed. He looked across at Father Francisco and smiled, his eyes glazing over. Father Francisco saw an inner calm wash over his friend.

Although Father Francisco had declined the blunt back then, even now at forty he felt a degree of regret. He thought of the film course for a moment as he turned the Kentucky Cheroot over in his hand.

'Fuck it,' he said aloud, pulling open the desk drawer. He took out the bag of marijuana and removed the insides of the cigar with the crucifix on his rosary, catching the loosened tobacco on the open pages of his bible. He filled the cigar with the marijuana.

'How bad can excommunication be?' he whispered, as he picked up his lighter.

First Funeral

Paul Beckman

Our mother sent my brother and me to sit next to our father. "Don't fidget," she said.

"He's already upset," I said. "He's sitting alone and crying."

"At least he loved your grandmother," she said.

My older brother (by one year) didn't speak to our father because he moved and left us. I didn't care because he only spoke to me to correct me or call me names.

"Mom says we should sit with you."

"Don't talk or fidget," he said.

"Can we breathe and cry?"

His look said it all.

Grandma was in a closed box at the head of the room. The funeral director, Robert L. Graves walked from the anti–room where the family was receiving visitors. The immediate family entered and took their seats in the front two rows.

A curtain parted behind Grandma and a string quartet played Russian music. My Aunt Lizzy, the only unmarried sister, walked over to us and spoke to my father. "Ben, it's not too late to make amends. Go to Lily."

My father didn't speak.

Director Graves said, "by request of the family". He pushed a button on the coffin and the top half opened.

Having recently seen a magician on the *Ed Sullivan Show*, I asked my brother if Director Graves was going to saw Grandma in half.

"Don't be stupid," my father said and got up to stand in line to see Grandma in her coffin. We followed him and he stood still in front for a long time, staring down. He then kissed the coffin.

My brother and I looked in at Grandma and I said, "She looks real," and my brother said, "She is real. Real dead." I reached in to touch her and my brother told me touching a dead person was a sin.

The quartet played a foxtrot. My father walked over to my mother and held out his hand. She paused, then took it and they danced beautifully around the coffin, down the aisle and back to my mother's seat where my father bowed and returned to his seat. My mother always said that for a big man, Dad was light on his feet. I asked Dad if he felt light on his feet when he danced with Mom. He shot me a look.

Director Graves introduced the Rabbi who spoke in Hebrew, English and threw in some Yiddish. He told stories about my grandfather leaving Russia, working and sending boat tickets for grandma and his parents. Gramps sat, tears running down his cheeks. None of the seven sisters spoke to each other until they got back to Grandpa's house and washed their hands with the pitcher and basin on the front stoop and then put the food out. Food loosened their tongues and they spoke to each other complimenting each dish, Mr. Graves, and the Rabbi. Dad never showed.

People left when the food was gone, and the Rabbi said his prayers. The next day everyone, including my grandfather, went back to work.

Mireille

Gary Percesepe

Her name was Mireille Bouchet and there is nothing much I can tell you. It's better to begin with Petal.

It seemed I was living another life inside my daily life when I went with Petal to the Whitney downtown and saw a strange art exhibit: water passing noisily through exposed PVC pipe, filling a large white plastic holding tank mounted overhead. Microphones amplified the humming water; graffiti covered the walls of the museum. Petal posed by the window, just before sunset. Below us, the Hudson River glimmered. I missed the shot. The sun had set. Her face was shadowed in the photo, her long pale neck invisible. I deleted the picture without showing her. We walked the Highline, above bars and restaurants long closed, unable to afford the rent, bookstores gobbled up by chains. Impossibly expensive Chanel handbags hung where poetry once sat dusty on a shelf. We passed places that held afterimages of former lovers, a party we attended, someone we owed money to. Returning to Gansevoort, we walked down Greenwich to Jane Street, crossed the West Side Highway and watched the lights of New Jersey blink on. We walked up Christopher Street, passing brownstones whose lit windows created a feeling of both presence and absence. Behind the glass pane the room was of course empty, but someone had left the light on. At night, New York is a city of hidden intentions. It was pointless to pose a question to Petal. No one ever answers questions. There was too much between us, which meant there was nothing at all. I watched her enter the small door of a parking garage on Horatio. It is always the same life that is lost, I thought.

Days later I was in France, doing research on the Situationist International. I was interested in tracing the movements of Guy Debord, who some believed responsible for the student uprising in May 1968 at the Sorbonne, and the wildcat strike that followed. He shunned publicity, and did his best to erase traces of his life. He spent most of his time in cafes, drinking. "Although I have read a lot," he said, "I have drunk even more. I have written much less than most people who write, but I have drunk much more than most people who drink." Debord made a film called 'Howls for Sade'. It concluded with these words: "Like lost children we live our unfinished lives." Perhaps it is more accurate to say that with these haunting words Debord *failed* to conclude his film, for what followed was twenty–four minutes of silence and a blindingly white screen. The film had vanished. In the most literal sense, "lost children" meant soldiers chosen for impossible missions, the kind no one returns from. But the term evokes an entire sphere of oblivion—what I have lost of myself, the time that has gone, the general evanescence of things. How is it possible to lose one's childhood, to turn one's back on it? Debord mentions nothing of the first twenty years of his life. Lost children come into the world disavowing the childhood they are given, yet one is never lost alone. There is a line in one of his books that fascinated me: *My method will be very simple; I will tell what I have loved.*

I rode a train into Paris. The train rushed too fast to read the name of the town. A woman entered my car and stood by the window, watching.

Mireille slouched beside the door of the train and asked my name. John, I lied. You're a writer, she said. How did you know that, I asked. You lied about your name, she said. We walked Rue Montparnasse, and turned into a side street. At the lower end of Rue d'Odessa a heavy rain began to fall. We took cover in the lobby of the Montparnasse cinema and found seats in the back. At intermission we had no idea what movie was playing. We returned to the street and walked past a Metro grate, the unmistakable whiff of ozone. We hurried to cross the street. At Rue Monge the pavement gave way to hard packed dirt. Puddles of rainwater splashed up, soiling our shoes. A black skyscraper, barely finished, rose menacingly higher as we walked toward it, diminished as we walked away. The head−lamp of a car illumined Mireille's face. She was no more than a spot of light without relief, an overexposed photograph. Near the Val−de−Grâce hospital she had taken my arm. It was very late.

A hotel. Its glass door was open, soft light in the lobby. A large dog lay in the middle of the lobby, asleep. The dog's chin rested on its paws above the dirty tile floor. Behind the reception desk a man, quite bald, thumbed the pages of an architecture magazine. I don't remember who led the way. We stepped lightly over the dog, not waking it. Calmly, we walked upstairs. A room covered in shadows, partially lit by a flickering corner lamppost filtered through a filthy curtain. There was a small table lamp and I lit it. I drew the curtain. She asked me to undress and then she undressed herself. Her wrists were small and graceful. She confided in me, hesitating in places, but not stopping, the way the truest encounters can take place between two people who know nothing of each other. A clock in the room chimed each half hour. The dog barked once, below. I felt as if I were outside Paris. Just before daybreak, the sound of horse hooves clip clopped on the dark street.

Many years later, walking near the Val–de–Grâce hospital, I tried to find the hotel. I hadn't written the name or even the address in my notebook, in that way we fail to record the most intimate details of our lives for fear that once recorded, fixed on paper, they will never be ours.

10 years of publishing
books listed from #99 to #1
(the book you are holding is #100)
in paperback and eBook

from Truth Serum Press,
Pure Slush Books and Everytime Press

find them all at
bequempublishing.com/shop/

truthserumpress.net/catalogue
pureslush.com/store
everytimepress.com/everytime-press-catalogue

Books published in 2020

 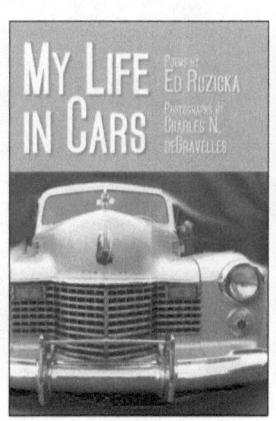 

• *The Last Summer of Hair* by Paul Ransom
978-1-922427-14-4 (paperback) 978-1-922427-15-1 (eBook)
• *My Life in Cars* by Ed Ruzicka
978-1-922427-10-6 (paperback) 978-1-922427-11-3 (eBook)
• *Wrong Way Go Back Pure Slush Vol. 19*
978-1-922427-06-9 (paperback) 978-1-922427-07-6 (eBook)

Books published in 2020

- *School Daze* by Irene Buckler
  978-1-922427-16-8 (paperback only)
- *Glow* *Truth Serum Vol. 6*
  978-1-922427-12-0 (paperback) 978-1-922427-13-7 (eBook)
- *The Tyranny of Bacon* *Pure Slush Vol. 18*
  978-1-922427-02-1 (paperback) 978-1-922427-03-8 (eBook)

- *Decennia* by Jan Chronister
  978-1-925536-98-0 (paperback) 978-1-925536-99-7 (eBook)
- *Perro Callejero (Stray Dog)* by Darren Howman
  978-1-925536-96-6 (paperback) 978-1-925536-97-3 (eBook)
- *Verdant* *Truth Serum Vol. 5*
  978-1-922427-04-5 (paperback) 978-1-922427-05-2 (eBook)

Books published in 2020

- *Sydneyside Reflections* by Mark Crimmins
978-1-925536-07-2 (paperback) 978-1-925536-08-9 (eBook)
- *How to Catch Flathead* by Peter Michal
978-1-925536-94-2 (paperback) 978-1-925536-95-9 (eBook)
- *The Beautifullest Pure Slush Vol. 17*
978-1-925536-23-2 (paperback) 978-1-925536-24-9 (eBook)

- *Indigomania Truth Serum Vol. 4*
978-1-925536-03-4 (paperback) 978-1-925536-84-3 (eBook)
- *Filthy Sucre* by Nod Ghosh
978-1-925536-92-8 (paperback) 978-1-925536-93-5
- *The Shitlist Pure Slush Vol. 16*
978-1-925536-90-4 (paperback) 978-1-925536-91-1 (eBook)

Books published in 2020 and 2019

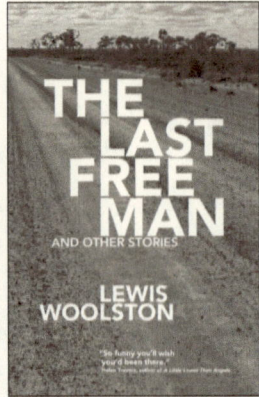

- *A Short Walk to the Sea* by Eddy Knight
  978-1-925536-01-1 (paperback) 978-1-925536-02-7 (eBook)
- *The Last Free Man and Other Stories* by Lewis Woolston
  978-1-925536-88-1 (paperback) 978-1-925536-89-8 (eBook)
- *The Pointless Revolution!* by Paul Ransom
  978-1-925536-74-4 (paperback) 978-1-925536-75-1 (eBook)

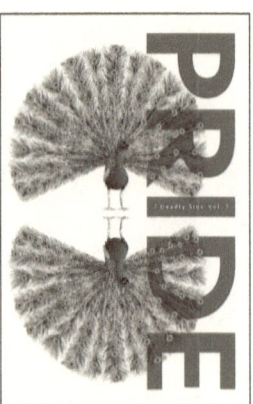

- *Easy Money and Other Stories* by Steve Evans
  978-1-925536-81-2 (paperback) 978-1-925536-82-9 (eBook)
- *Stories My Gay Uncle Told Me Truth Serum Vol. 3*
  978-1-925536-86-7 (paperback) 978-1-925536-87-4 (eBook)
- *Pride 7 Deadly Sins Vol. 7*
  978-1-925536-72-0 (paperback) 978-1-925536-73-7 (eBook)

Books published in 2019 and 2018

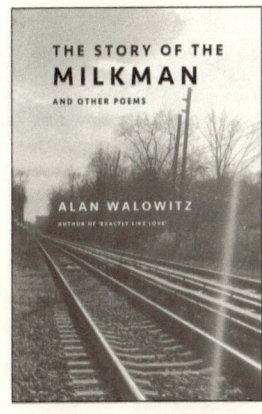  

- *The Story of the Milkman and Other Poems* by Alan Walowitz
  978-1-925536-76-8 (paperback) 978-1-925536-77-5 (eBook)
- *Minotaur and Other Stories* by Salvatore Difalco
  978-1-925536-79-9 (paperback) 978-1-925536-80-5 (eBook)
- *Envy 7 Deadly Sins Vol. 6*
  978-1-925536-70-6 (paperback) 978-1-925536-71-3 (eBook)

 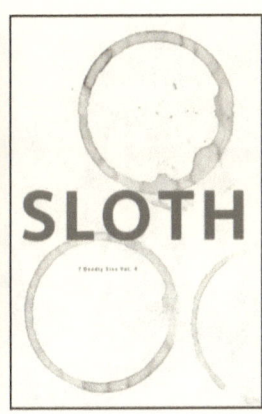 

- *Wrath 7 Deadly Sins Vol. 5*
  978-1-925536-68-3 (paperback) 978-1-925536-69-0 (eBook)
- *Sloth 7 Deadly Sins Vol. 4*
  978-1-925536-66-9 (paperback) 978-1-925536-67-6 (eBook)
- *The In-Betweens* by Davon Loeb
  978-1-925536-56-0 (paperback) 978-1-925536-57-7 (eBook)

Books published in 2018

- *The Book of Acrostics* by John Lambremont Sr.
  978-1-925536-52-2 (paperback) 978-1-925536-53-9 (eBook)
- *Square Pegs* by Rob Walker
  978-1-925536-62-1 (paperback) 978-1-925536-63-8 (eBook)
- *Cheat Sheets* by Edward O'Dwyer
  978-1-925536-60-7 (paperback) 978-1-925536-61-4 (eBook)

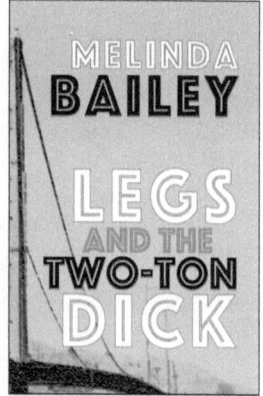

- *Greed 7 Deadly Sins Vol. 3*
  978-1-925536-64-5 (paperback) 978-1-925536-65-2 (eBook)
- *The Crazed Wind* by Nod Ghosh
  978-1-925536-58-4 (paperback) 978-1-925536-59-1 (eBook)
- *Legs and the Two-Ton Dick* by Melinda Bailey
  978-1-925536-37-9 (paperback) 978-1-925536-38-6 (eBook)

Books published in 2018

- *Gluttony 7 Deadly Sins Vol. 2*
978-1-925536-54-6 (paperback) 978-1-925536-55-3 (eBook)
- *Lenin's Asylum* by A. A. Weiss
978-1-925536-50-8 (paperback) 978-1-925536-51-5 (eBook)
- *Dollhouse Masquerade* by Samuel E. Cole
978-1-925536-43-0 (paperback) 978-1-925536-44-7 (eBook)

- *It's About the Dog* by Guilie Castillo Oriard
978-1-925536-19-5 (paperback) 978-1-925536-20-1 (eBook)
- *Lust 7 Deadly Sins Vol. 1*
978-1-925536-47-8 (paperback) / 978-1-925536-48-5 (eBook)
- *Kiss Kiss* by Paul Beckman
978-1-925536-21-8 (paperback) 978-1-925536-22-5 (eBook)

Books published in 2018 and 2017

• *Inklings* by Irene Buckler
978-1-925536-41-6 (paperback) 978-1-925536-42-3 (eBook)
• *On the Bitch* by Matt Potter
978-1-925536-45-4 (paperback) 978-1-925536-46-1 (eBook)
• *Happy² Pure Slush Vol. 15*
978-1-925536-39-3 (paperback) 978-1-925536-40-9 (eBook)

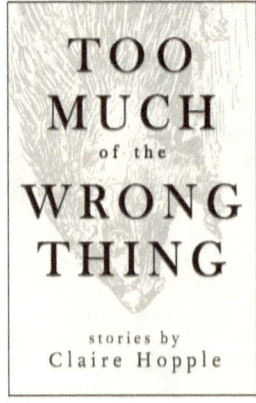  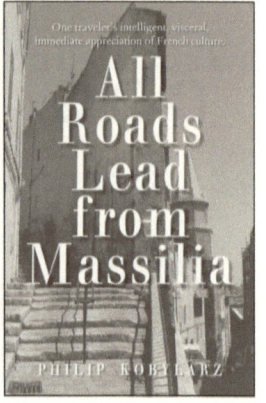

• *Too Much of the Wrong Thing* by Claire Hopple
978-1-925536-33-1 (paperback) 978-1-925536-34-8 (eBook)
• *Track Tales* by Mercedes Webb-Pullman
978-1-925536-35-5 (paperback) 978-1-925536-36-2 (eBook)
• *All Roads Lead from Massilia* by Philip Kobylarz
978-1-925536-27-0 (paperback) 978-1-925536-28-7 (eBook)

Books published in 2017 and 2016

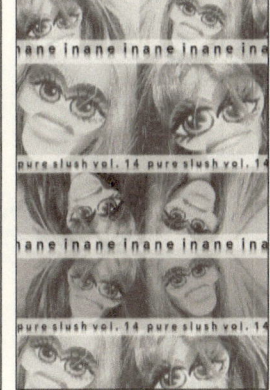

- *Wiser Truth Serum Vol. 2*
978-1-925101-31-7 (paperback) 978-1-925101-32-4 (eBook)
- *Inane Pure Slush Vol. 14*
978-1-925536-17-1 (paperback) 978-1-925536-18-8 (eBook)
- *Luck and Other Truths* by Richard Mark Glover
978-1-925101-77-5 (paperback) 978-1-925536-04-1 (eBook)

- *True Truth Serum Vol. 1*
978-1-925101-29-4 (paperback) 978-1-925101-30-0 (eBook)
- *Hello Berlin!* by Jason S. Andrews
978-1-925536-11-9 (paperback) 978-1-925536-12-6 (eBook)
- *Freak Pure Slush Vol. 13*
978-1-925536-16-4 (paperback) 978-1-925536-15-7 (eBook)

Books published in 2016

  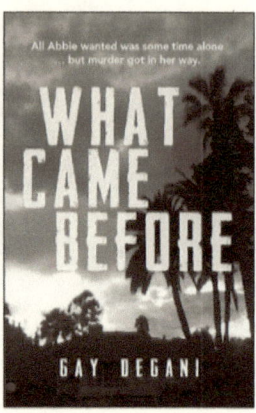

• *Deer Michigan* by Jack C. Buck
978-1-925536-25-6 (paperback) 978-1-925536-26-3 (eBook)
• *Summer Pure Slush Vol. 12*
978-1-925536-13-3 (paperback) 978-1-925536-14-0 (eBook)
• *What Came Before* by Gay Degani
978-1-925536-05-8 (paperback) 978-1-925536-06-5 (eBook)

• *Rain Check* by Levi Andrew Noe
978-1-925536-09-6 (paperback) 978-1-925536-10-2 (eBook)
• *tall…ish Pure Slush Vol. 11*
978-1-925101-80-5 (paperback) 978-1-925101-98-0 (eBook)
• *a whiteboard, a marker and this book! #2* by Matt Potter
978-1-925101-96-6 (paperback only)

Books published 2016 and 2015

- *a whiteboard, a marker and this book! #1* by Matt Potter
  978-1-925101-82-9 (paperback only)
- *Based on True Stories* by Matt Potter
  978-1-925101-75-1 (paperback) 978-1-925101-76-8 (eBook)
- *dear Petrov* by Susan Tepper
  (no longer in print)

  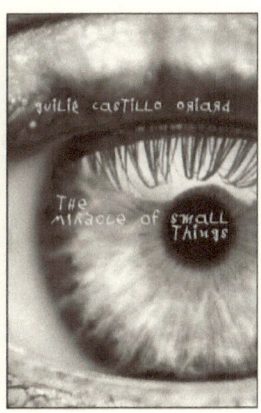

- *Five Pure Slush Vol. 10*
  978-1-925101-71-3 (paperback) 978-1-925101-72-0 (eBook)
- *Rattle of Want* by Gay Degani
  978-1-925101-67-6 (paperback) 978-1-925101-68-3 (eBook)
- *The Miracle of Small Things* by Guilie Castillo Oriard
  978-1-925101-73-7 (paperback) 978-1-925101-74-4 (eBook)

Books published in 2015 and 2014

- *La Ronde* by Townsend Walker
978-1-925101-64-5 (paperback) 978-1-925101-65-2 (eBook)
- *Feast! Pure Slush Vol. 9*
978-1-925101-63-8 (paperback) 978-1-925101-66-9 (eBook)
- *2014 October November December*
978-1-925101-48-5 (paperback only)

- *2014 July August September*
978-1-925101-47-8 (paperback only)
- *2014 April May June*
978-1-925101-46-1 (paperback only)
- *2014 January February March*
978-1-925101-33-1 (paperback only)

Books published in 2014

- *The Vixen Scream and other Bible Stories* by Nancy Stohlman
  978-1-925101-11-9 (paperback) 978-1-925101-12-6 (eBook)
- *Many Fish to Fry* by Abha Iyengar
  978-1-925101-59-1 (paperback) 978-1-925101-60-7 (eBook)
- *2014 December Vol. 12*
  978-1-925101-56-0 (paperback) 978-1-925101-57-7 (eBook)

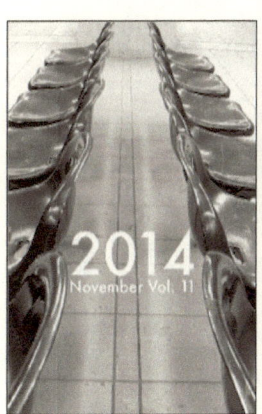  

- *2014 November Vol. 11*
  978-1-925101-53-9 (paperback) 978-1-925101-54-6 (eBook)
- *2014 October Vol. 10*
  978-1-925101-50-8 (paperback) 978-1-925101-51-5 (eBook)
- *2014 September Vol. 9*
  978-1-925101-43-0 (paperback) 978-1-925101-44-7 (eBook)

Books published in 2014

- *2014 August Vol. 8*
978-1-925101-40-9 (paperback) 978-1-925101-41-6 (eBook)
- *The Company of Men* by Luisa Brenta
978-1-925101-06-5 (paperback) 978-1-925101-09-6 (eBook)
- *2014 July Vol. 7*
978-1-925101-37-9 (paperback) 978-1-925101-38-6 (eBook)

- *2014 June Vol. 6*
978-1-925101-49-2 (paperback) 978-1-925101-35-5 (eBook)
- *2014 May Vol. 5*
978-1-925101-30-0 (paperback) 978-1-925101-32-4 (eBook)
- *2014 April Vol. 4*
978-1-925101-27-0 (paperback) 978-1-925101-28-7 (eBook)

Books published in 2014 and 2013

 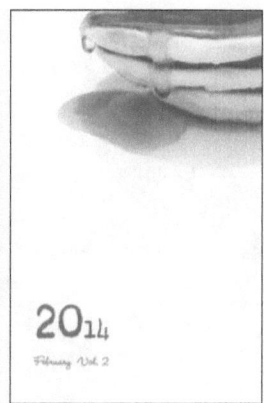 

- *2014 March Vol. 3*
978-1-925101-17-1 (paperback) 978-1-925101-18-8 (eBook)
- *2014 February Vol. 2*
978-1-925101-14-0 (paperback) 978-1-925101-15-7 (eBook)
- *2014 January Vol. 1*
978-1-925101-03-4 (paperback) 978-1-925101-04-1 (eBook)

- *itch* by Gary Percesepe
978-1-925101-21-8 (paperback) 978-1-925101-22-5 (eBook)
- *falling and other poems* by Gary Percesepe
978-1-925101-24-9 (paperback) 978-1-925101-25-6 (eBook)
- *barcode Pure Slush Vol. 8*
978-1-925101-00-3 (paperback) 978-1-925101-01-0 (eBook)

Books published in 2013

 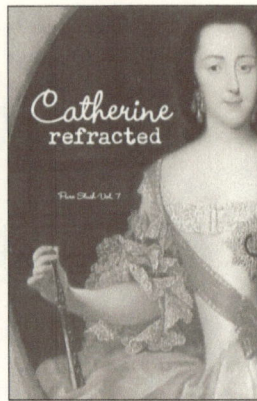 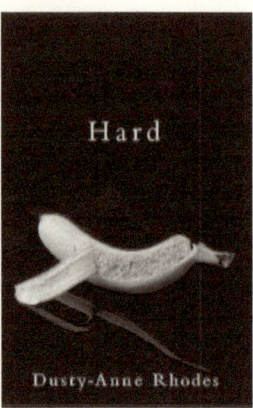

- *The Merrill Diaries* by Susan Tepper
(no longer in print)
- *Catherine refracted Pure Slush Vol. 7*
978-1-925101-78-2 (paperback) 978-1-925101-79-9 (eBook)
- *Hard* by Dusty-Anne Rhodes
978-1-291-37970-9 (paperback) 978-1-925101-81-2 (eBook)

 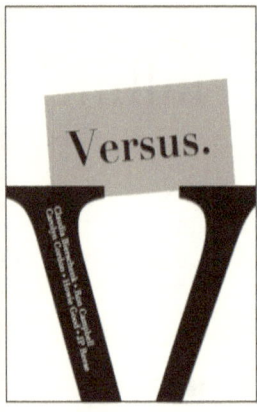 

- *obit. Pure Slush Vol. 6*
978-1-300-86001-3 (paperback) 978-1-925101-83-6 (eBook)
- *Versus. Pure Slush Vol. 5*
978-1-925101-84-3 (paperback) 978-1-925101-85-0 (eBook)
- *Glass Animals* by Stephen V. Ramey
978-1-925101-86-7 (paperback) 978-1-925101-87-4 (eBook)

Books published in 2012 and 2011

• *gorge: a novel in stories Pure Slush Vol. 4*
978-1-925101-88-1 (paperback) 978-1-925101-89-8 (eBook)
• *real Pure Slush Vol. 3*
978-1-925101-90-4 (paperback) 978-1-304-00328-7(eBook)
• *Wild* by Gill Hoffs
978-1-925101-92-8 (paperback) 978-1-925101-93-5 (eBook)

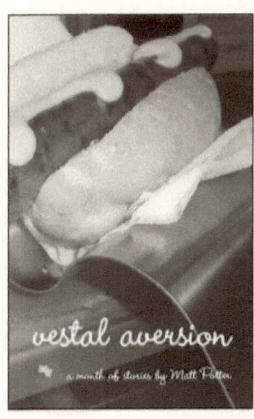  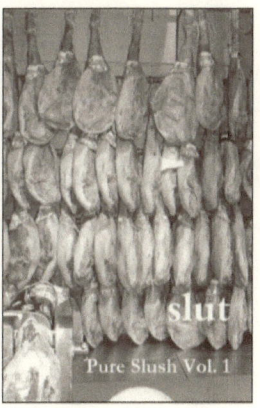

• *Vestal A version* by Matt Potter
978-1-925101-94-2 (paperback) 978-1-925101-95-9 (eBook)
• *Notausgang (emergency exit) Pure Slush Vol. 2*
978-1-4717-0059-0 (paperback) 978-1-925101-97-3 (eBook)
• *slut Pure Slush Vol. 1*
978-1-4716-0674-8 (paperback) 978-1-925101-99-7 (eBook)

www.ingramcontent.com/pod-product-compliance
Lightning Source LLC
Chambersburg PA
CBHW020843020726
47497CB00005B/1227